Praise for Brendan O'Carroll and his bestselling novel *The Mammy*

"Cheerful ... as unpretentious and satisfying as a home-cooked meal ... with a delicious dessert of an ending."
—*The New York Times Book Review*

"Irreverently comical ... Reads like Frank McCourt's *Angela's Ashes* on Prozac ... jaunty, charming ... It's refreshing to enter O'Carroll's fun-loving working-class Dublin world."
—*Entertainment Weekly*

"A heartwarming and very funny book."
—Roddy Doyle, author of *Paddy Clarke Ha Ha Ha* and *A Star Called Henry*

"How to lose weight: Read *The Mammy*. You will laugh your arse off and your tears will do away with your water retention problem. It is an uproariously funny account of growing up in inner-city Dublin— a laugh-out-loud book with a Dickensian twist to it."
—Malachy McCourt, author of *A Monk Swimming*

"An almost surefire winner ... one of those books that demand to be read in one sitting."
—*The Irish Voice*

The youngest of eleven children, BRENDAN O'CARROLL was born in North Dublin in 1955. An acclaimed playright and stand-up comedian, he is the creator of the popular Irish radio show, *Mrs. Browne's Boys*. *The Mammy*, the first novel in his bestselling Mrs. Browne trilogy, was the basis for the feature film *Agnes Browne*, directed by and starring Anjelica Huston. *The Chisellers* and *The Granny* are the second and final books in the trilogy. All three novels are available in Plume editions.

THE
GRANNY

Brendan O'Carroll

A PLUME BOOK

PLUME
Published by the Penguin Group
Penguin Putnam Inc., 375 Hudson Street, New York, New York 10014, U.S.A.
Penguin Books Ltd, 27 Wrights Lane, London W8 5TZ, England
Penguin Books Australia Ltd, Ringwood, Victoria, Australia
Penguin Books Canada Ltd, 10 Alcorn Avenue, Toronto, Ontario,
Canada M4V 3B2
Penguin Books (N.Z.) Ltd, 182–190 Wairau Road, Auckland 10,
New Zealand

Penguin Books Ltd, Registered Offices: Harmondsworth,
Middlesex, England

Published by Plume, a member of Penguin Putnam Inc. Originally
published in Ireland by The O'Brien Press.

First American Printing, August 2000
10 9 8 7 6 5 4 3

Ⓟ REGISTERED TRADEMARK—MARCA REGISTRADA

LIBRARY OF CONGRESS CATALOGING-IN-PUBLICATION DATA
O'Carroll, Brendan.
    The granny / Brendan O'Carroll.
        p.   cm.
    ISBN 0-452-28184-9
        1. Grandmothers—Ireland—Fiction. 2. Women—Ireland—Fiction.
3. Dublin (Ireland)—Fiction. I. Title.
PR6065.C36 G73 2000
823'.914—dc21

99-089125

Printed in the United States of America

PUBLISHER'S NOTE
This is a work of fiction. Names, characters, places, and incidents are either
the product of the author's imagination or are used fictitiously, and any
resemblance to actual persons, living or dead, business establishments,
events, or locales is entirely coincidental.

To say hello to
Sarah-Mary Browne

and to say farewell to
Rita Fitzsimons
I miss you more than words can say

Introduction

Somebody up there loves me? My delight at seeing *The Chisellers* at number one in the bestsellers list was matched only by seeing *The Mammy* right behind it in the number two spot. Thank you from the bottom of my heart. The day before *The Chisellers* was launched I made my debut as a playwright, director and actor in the Tivoli Theatre in Francis Street with *The Course*. I cannot tell you how hard I worked on that play. When the Dublin Theatre Festival rejected it I was gutted. I sat down and read the play again, and again. The play is funny. I tried to see what it was that they were rejecting but I couldn't. Despite warnings of doom and gloom from those who believe they know what you all like, we went ahead and produced the play. It has broken all box-office records since. Somebody up there loves me? No. It's not somebody up there. It's YOU. Make no mistake, you have done this.

I try never to forget the great swell of support and help I receive from the wonderful people I have around me – Tommy Swarbrigg, Tom Bluett, Shay Fitzsimons, Dermot O'Neill, Evelyn Conway, Mary Cullen, Jimmy Staunton, Ashley Browne, Alan Kelly, Dorothy Yelverton, Jenny Gibney, Brendan Morrissey, Esther Doorley, Niall Murray, Annette Dolan and Mike Pyatt. From the building of a set for the play to finding a cotton bud just when it's needed, each and every one of these people has gone the extra mile. Let me please acknowledge now how much you all have enriched my life, and that of my family, by becoming a part of it. I love you.

I have, of course, kept a special place for Gerry Browne. Someday he will write his own book, or else I will pen his story. Then you will all know this kind, warm, hard-working, unselfish and wonderful man that I am so proud to stand beside and say, *this* is my friend.

For my wife Doreen I have left this final paragraph, to say only this: I have made so many mistakes in my life that it would be impossible to count them. But asking you to dance with me twenty-seven years ago certainly wasn't one of them. Thanks for all you have given.

Brendan O'Carroll
July 1996

Chapter 1

ROTUNDA MATERNITY HOSPITAL

AGNES BROWNE WAS NO STRANGER to childbirth. Within fourteen years of marrying her now deceased husband Redser, she had given birth to seven children. But that was when she was between twenty and thirty-four years of age, young and fit. Now, at forty-seven, she wasn't able for it. With her eyes tightly closed and her fists clenched, she took a huge breath and let it out in short bursts, 'Ssst, ssst, ssst, ssst, ssst, ssst,' ending with a soft moan.

Her son Dermot, one of her twins – her fourth delivery and now twenty-five years of age – leaned close to her ear to speak. 'Mammy, for fuck sake will yeh stop,' he whispered.

'That's easy for you to say, Dermot, you have no idea what childbirth is like,' she answered through clenched teeth.

'I'll take your word for it, Mammy. Now give it up. People are staring at us!'

Dermot was right. Besides Agnes, her sons Rory, Dermot and Trevor, and her daughter Cathy, there were ten complete strangers in the waiting room. Every eye was staring in wonderment at this woman in a headscarf and trench coat holding a huge bag of fruit on her lap and going through the motions of childbirth.

Dermot's comment prompted Agnes to open her eyes and she glanced at the strangers, all of whom immediately found things on the walls, ceiling and floor to look at. Agnes gathered herself together and sat up straighter. As she did this a melon rolled out of the bag of fruit and landed square between her feet with a thud. Everybody jumped. The room was silent for a moment as they all stared at the melon. Suddenly everyone erupted in spontaneous laughter.

'Congratulations, Mammy, we'll call him Pip,' Dermot announced, and again the room broke up with laughter.

The door of the waiting room opened and the laughter stopped. In through the doorway peered the head of Ward Sister Mary Sheridan. She looked around with a scowl on her face. Now everybody was staring at the floor or the walls and trying desperately to act innocent. The Ward Sister said nothing and closed the door.

'My Jesus, did yeh see the face on that one?' Agnes asked this question of the entire room. Nobody answered. 'I wouldn't say she ever needs to buy yogurt, she just gets a pint of milk and stares at it.'

Once again everyone in the room laughed, but this time they either covered their faces or laughed through their nostrils so as not to be as noisy. When the laughter died the room once again fell into silence. After a couple of minutes Agnes suddenly stood up.

'Nobody tells yeh anythin' in this bloody hospital,' she announced.

'Mammy, sit down. If there's any news they'll come in and tell us,' Rory Browne said to his mother.

Agnes thought for a moment and then suddenly said, 'I'm goin' out to ask. That's my son's wife in there and I'm entitled to know,' and with that she left the room.

* * *

Mark Browne dabbed Betty's forehead with a cool, damp cloth. Betty lay motionless, her eyes closed. She was resting between contractions. The last contraction had been particularly long and painful. With the feel of the cool cloth across her forehead and down her cheek Betty smiled and opened her eyes to see Mark's smiling face looking down at her. She squeezed his hand.

'I'm not doin' very well, am I?' Betty spoke in a weak voice.

'You're doin' great,' Mark answered quickly.

'Thanks.'

Mark once again dipped the cloth in the cool water, squeezed it out and began to dab Betty's face. 'Everybody's outside in the waitin' room, except Simon – he's up in your mother's waitin' for her to come back.' Betty's mother was away on a pilgrimage at Knock that day. Her prayers were for a short labour for her daughter and the birth of a baby girl.

Betty smiled at the thought of the Browne family sitting out in the waiting room. 'It's a wonder your Mammy isn't in here with us cheerin' me on,' she said.

They both laughed. But no sooner had Betty spoken than from behind Mark she saw the delivery room door open slightly and Agnes Browne's head, wrapped in her headscarf, dart through. Agnes's head bobbed as she tried to check behind the screens around each of the beds in the delivery room.

11

'Jesus Christ!' Betty exclaimed as she turned her head away from the door. Too late – Agnes had spotted her.

'Yo hoo, Betty! I have some fruit for yeh!' Agnes called quietly and with a lilt in her voice.

Mark swung around. 'Mammy, for God's sake get out,' he snapped, 'you're not allowed in here.'

Before he had finished speaking Agnes was confronted by Nurse Mary Sheridan who blocked Agnes's view of the bed and simply said, 'Out.'

'I'm just checkin' –'

'Out.'

'Just lettin' her know we're all here.'

'Out!' Nurse Sheridan opened the door and, gripping Agnes's coat, began to usher her out into the corridor. But not before Agnes waved goodbye to Betty with the advice, 'Don't push till they tell yeh, Betty. See yeh later.'

Out in the corridor Agnes straightened her coat under the stare of Nurse Sheridan.

'I just wanted to give her some mortal support,' Agnes said by way of explanation.

'I'm sure she's delighted. Now, Mrs Browne, stay out of there, all right?' Nurse Sheridan turned her back and went to re-enter the delivery room.

Agnes called after her. 'Nurse, how's she doin', really?'

Although Nurse Sheridan was annoyed at Agnes's intrusion, she could hear the genuine concern in the woman's voice and she softened a little.

'She's doing well, Mrs Browne. She's got a bit to go yet, but still, she's seven centimetres.' Nurse Sheridan turned and was gone, leaving a puzzled Agnes behind in the corridor.

Agnes re-entered the waiting room and with an air of authority walked back and took her seat. As she did so she was followed by every head in the room. For a few moments Agnes sat quietly.

'Well?' asked Dermot.

'Well what?' Agnes answered very smugly.

'How is she?'

'Oh, I'm very pleased with her, she's doin' well,' Agnes answered as if she had personally examined Betty. 'Although she has a bit to go yet, about seven litres.'

'Seven litres? What does that mean?' Dermot asked.

'Oh, it's a gynaecological term, Dermot, you wouldn't understand,' Agnes brushed off the question and extracted her packet of cigarettes from her handbag.

Two hours later there was still no news. Dermot had gone down to the newsagent's across the road from the hospital and bought a deck of cards. Now he, Rory, Trevor and one of the other men who had been waiting for hours in the waiting room were sitting in a corner playing Don.

Agnes was staring across the room at a young man who spent the whole time biting his nails. Agnes was thinking that if this man's wife didn't have her child soon he'd have chewed his hand off. At this point the man looked up and caught Agnes's eye. He smiled and she smiled back.

'Is it your first?' she asked.

'Yeh.'

'Ah that's nice. Is she long in there?' Agnes asked, nodding towards the door.

'Four hours.'

'Don't be worryin', son. The first is the longest. Oh don't remind me! On me first – Mark, that's the baby's father inside – I was ninety-six hours in labour.'

13

The man's eyes opened wide and he gave a short, silent gasp.

The man playing Don in the corner with Mrs Browne's three sons muttered softly, 'Ninety-six fuckin' hours!'

Dermot smiled. 'Don't mind what she's sayin'. The first time I heard her tellin' that story it was sixteen hours. Jaysus, by the time I'm havin' a child she'll be sittin' in the waiting room tellin' everyone that she was so long in labour that Mark was born with a moustache.'

The four men laughed. Agnes eyed them suspiciously.

Finally the door of the waiting room opened slowly and in walked a dazed Mark Browne. His blue eyes were glazed and he had a smile on his face from ear to ear. Nobody moved. Mark looked over at his mother and his eyes cleared as if he had suddenly woken up. He could see the question in her face.

'It's a boy,' he said simply.

Agnes and Cathy threw their arms around Mark and hugged him warmly as tears streamed down their faces. Trevor, Dermot and Rory jumped up simultaneously, sending playing cards scattering across the room. They first congratulated their brother and then they began to congratulate each other. Just in the nick of time, it seemed, Simon and Mrs Collins, Betty's mother, entered the waiting room.

'It's a boy,' the Browne family all announced together.

Thirty minutes later the Browne family and Mrs Collins stood in a semi-circle around the baby crib at the bottom of Betty's bed, their eyes glowing with pride as they beheld the newest Browne to enter the world. Betty Browne sat propped up by four pillows, sipping a cup of hot tea. She was delighted with her new offspring and thrilled that the event should bring so much joy to so many people. Her smile beamed. Agnes looked at Betty and she too was smiling in delight. Betty gave her a wink.

'Where's Mark?' Agnes asked.

Betty pointed at the door. 'Gone to the toilet.'

'I think I need to go meself,' said Agnes, 'the excitement is killin' me.'

She got to the door of the Ladies just as the door of the Gents on the opposite side of the corridor opened and Mark stepped out.

'Are yeh all right, Mammy?'

Agnes turned and smiled at her eldest son, as proud of him as she always had been. She walked over to him and placed her hands on his shoulders.

'I'm fine, Mark, and I'm so, so happy for yeh, son.'

'And I'm happy for you – Granny!' Mark grinned, and turned back towards the ward.

Agnes stood in the hallway for a moment. Granny? *Granny!*

The word fell like a sack of coal across Agnes's back. She felt her shoulders dip and her spine bend. For some inexplicable reason she hadn't thought about it like that at all. She looked down at the back of her left hand – it looked wrinkled and her wedding ring seemed to sink into the flesh of her fourth finger. For the first time in her life Agnes Browne felt old.

Chapter 2

SENGA SOFT FURNISHINGS LIMITED and its new Managing Director, Mark Browne, had been very good to each other. In the years following former owner Mr Wise's demise, Mark had not just reorganised, but had completely refurbished the factory. Gone were the old belt-driven bandsaws and chain-driven drills. The factory now boasted a complete range of high-tech, compact, fast and accurate machines. The new machinery was essential, as the factory now turned out furniture in numbers greater than even Mark had anticipated. The client list for Senga Furnishings now read like a who's who in the department store directory of Ireland and the United Kingdom. Mark's flair for design and his hard work were handsomely rewarded with a new semi-detached home in Baldoyle, just a mile or so from Dublin's beautiful golden coastline. Strangely enough, Mark remained the only Browne to work at Senga Furnishings. Each of the boys and Cathy decided to go their own way in life, to strike out and do their own thing, an independent streak they had all inherited from their mother.

*   *   *

Seven days after the birth of his child, Mark arrived at the Rotunda Hospital in the company Ford Cortina to take Betty, babe-in-arms, home to what was usually a peaceful house. Not today, however! The entire Browne clan, along with Mrs Collins, were waiting at Mark's house. The pink-faced little child with the big brown eyes was greeted with a barrage of Oohs and Aahs as ten pairs of eyes ogled him.

What began as a family reception for the new child soon turned into a celebration, and by early evening had turned into a noisy party. So much so that Betty and Mrs Collins decided to slip away with the baby, and the new child spent his first night out of hospital in his Nanna Collins's flat while the Browne clan partied on into the early hours.

In the week since the birth there was not a conversation in the Browne household that did not eventually turn to what the first Browne grandchild should be named. Agnes was plugging for Gerard, a name she had wanted for Mark when he was born, but had lost the battle to her husband Redser. Dermot fancied James, after the soul singer James Brown. Between the rest of the family names like Jason, Peter, William, and Rory's choice of Gabriel, received various peaks of popularity. Of course, the final choice would be down to Mark and Betty. This is why the morning following the child's homecoming Agnes stared across the breakfast table at Dermot with a shocked expression.

'Arrow? They can't be fuckin' serious.'

Agnes was stunned by Dermot's revelation. She filled the kettle, repeating the name, her head still woozy from the cider the night before. She had come down twice during the night to take huge mouthfuls from the pint of cool water she kept in the fridge. Each time she opened the door the light from the fridge seemed like a prison search light, and her head rattled. She had been feeling a

17

little better until Dermot brought up the subject of the child's name.

'That's what Mark told me,' he confirmed.

'Yeh can't call a baby Arrow – he's not a fuckin' Apache, for God's sake.' Agnes was incredulous.

The two sat in silence. The element in the kettle began to heat and the water surrounding it began to complain. Agnes spoke her thoughts aloud again.

'Arrow Browne. In school he'll be registered as: Browne, Arrow! Good God, it sounds like somethin' a cowboy might find up his arse!'

Dermot laughed but Agnes glared at him; she hadn't meant to be funny. So he returned to silent contemplation, and this is how Rory found them when he came down.

'What's up?' he asked.

It was Dermot who answered. 'Mark and Betty are callin' the baby Arrow.'

'Ha! That's great. If he grows up and marries Bo Derek we'll have a Bow and Arrow in the family,' Rory joked.

The two young men burst into laughter.

'It's not funny.' Agnes brought the laughter to a halt. 'Arrow Browne! What'll people think? Can you imagine the christening – the priest pourin' the water and sayin': I christen this child Arrow. I'll be mortified.'

*   *   *

The christening day was a great affair. After the church service everybody headed down to the city centre to Foley's pub, the venue for virtually every Browne family celebration for twenty-seven years. Mr Foley had prepared cocktail sausages and little squares of cheese on cocktail sticks. Everybody was dressed in their Sunday best and after the preliminary niceties the evening broke into a singsong. Agnes sang 'The Wonder of You', and accused the band of being three beats behind her. The whole old Jarro neighbourhood, where the Brownes had spent their childhood, was having a great time. Mark moved from table to table, thanking everyone for coming and for the lovely christening gifts. He spied his mother at the bar buying a drink for herself and her boyfriend Pierre, and made his way over to her.

'There yeh are, Ma.'

Agnes spun around on hearing her eldest son's voice. 'Ah Mark, love.' She gave him a huge hug.

'Enjoying yourself, Mammy?' He asked, chuckling.

'What's the giggle for?' Agnes asked with one eyebrow raised.

'You and the baby's name.' Mark began to laugh.

Agnes reddened a little. 'Oh yes, well, how d'yeh pronounce it again?'

'Aaron! It's from the Bible.'

'Aaron from the Bible – I love it!'

Agnes was thrilled. *Anything* was better than Arrow. In the background a glass was being banged off a table and Agnes and Mark turned to see Pierre standing and holding his hand in the air for silence.

'Here we go again, another fuckin' speech,' Agnes moaned.

Mark just laughed. 'Ah leave him to it, Ma, he enjoys them.'

Silence fell over the room.

'I would like to make a speech,' Pierre began, although it came out like, 'Ah wood lik to mik a spitch,' as his French accent was still very thick.

There was a great cheer from the crowd. When the room fell into silence again Pierre went on.

'All of today you have congratulated Betty, the new mother, Mark, the new father, and of course Aaron, the newest child of the Browne family.'

This was met with a huge cheer. Pierre again held his hand in the air. 'But now I would like to propose a toast.'

Buster Brady turned to Dermot and asked, 'What's a fuckin' tist?'

'Toast, he means a *toast* – shut up, Buster.'

Buster shut up, Pierre went on. 'To the beautiful Agnes Browne.' All the glasses were raised and Agnes beamed a smile, but Pierre wasn't finished. 'Welcome, *Granny*!'

There was a loud cheer. Agnes held her smile, but through her teeth she said, 'Sit the fuck down, Pierre.'

Pierre did and as he did he took Agnes's arm and pushed her up to acknowledge the toast. She raised her glass and looked around the room. There they all were, Agnes's little orphans, all adults now. Her entire brood, except for poor Frankie – but at this moment Agnes wouldn't let herself think about her one stray son who had come to a no-good end. Mark settled and married to Betty and with a beautiful young son; Rory with his friend Dino, both now top hair stylists at Wash & Blow; Trevor, one year to go in art college, and soon to be a qualified graphic artist; Simon, now head porter in St Patrick's Hospital; Cathy there with her fiancé Mick O'Leary; and Dermot there with ...? Suddenly Agnes's expression changed. The crowd roared in unison, 'Congratulations, Granny!' and everyone tossed their drink back. The roar and the action of the drinking served to hide Agnes's change of expression.

What had caused Agnes to look worried was that Dermot was there with Mary Carter. Agnes knew the Carter family well – Jack Carter, Mary's father, had left their home in Townsend Street one morning ten years ago and was never seen again; Helen Carter proceeded to drink herself into oblivion and the children reared themselves on the streets of Dublin. Agnes felt sorry for the family, particularly the children, but her pity didn't extend to accepting Mary Carter, now a known junkie, and, Agnes suspected, a drug pusher, into the Browne family. She had warned Dermot weeks ago, but he had said it was just a casual affair and it would come to nothing at all.

Dermot *had* noticed his mother's change of expression and when at last he caught her eye he gave her a smile and a wink, indicating that she should not worry, everything was okay. Agnes's tension eased and she returned his smile.

It was Dino Doyle, Rory's friend, who noticed how sombre Trevor had been all evening. When he said it to Rory, Rory sought out Trevor in an effort to find out what was bothering him. He found him standing beneath the switched-off television, resting his elbow on the cigarette machine, alone.

'Hi, Trevor, great isn't it?' Rory beamed a smile at Trevor.

'Yeh, great.'

'Are you all right, Trevor? You seem a bit down.'

Trevor brightened slightly. 'No, I'm grand, Rory, just a little tired – yeh know, exams comin' up and all that.'

'Can I get you a drink?'

'No, you're all right, Rory, you go on back to Dino. You don't want to leave him roamin' around here on his own – he might find somebody else!'

'If he does they'll be holdin' a white stick.' Both the brothers burst out laughing and Rory kissed Trevor on the cheek and went back to Dino. Trevor took another sip from his drink and his thoughts once again turned to Maria Nicholson.

Trevor was by far the quietest and shyest of the Brownes. Although as an artist his work was tremendously expressive, when it came to communicating verbally, especially on a one-to-one basis, his mind went blank, his mouth went dry and he would always beat a retreat as quickly as possible. In the past it had not been a real problem for Trevor as he was quite happy with his own company, but lately it had become the source of great pain. The cause of the pain was Maria Nicholson.

Maria had joined the College of Art and Design, where Trevor attended, just one year ago. She had transferred there from Vancouver in Canada. Although she was Irish-born, from Limerick city in fact, her father was a design engineer specialising in bridges, and his work took him all over the world. Wherever Daddy had travelled, the family had travelled. Maria was thrilled to be back in Ireland, and although a late student when entering fourth year, she was readily accepted by all. She attended only two classes with Trevor – Art History and Graphic Design. But from the very first moment Trevor Browne had laid eyes on her he knew he was in love. Trevor made several attempts to speak to Maria but each time not a single word would come out from his mouth. She would tilt her head sideways, tap him on the shoulder and say, 'Look, I'll talk to you later, okay?' and be gone.

So Trevor had made a decision. He would communicate with her through his art. One day during a free class, Trevor took a length of artist's canvas and cut it into fourteen squares, each square two and a half inches by two and a half inches. At home in his bedroom he set the first tiny canvas on an easel and began to paint with oils. His plan was to paint a miniature copy of works of great artists, signing each miniature with the first letter of the artist's name. Each letter would correspond to a letter in Maria Nicholson's name. Each miniature took two weeks to complete, and as each one was completed he made a little frame for it, parcelled it and left it somewhere that Maria would find it. Tied to the tiny parcel was a tiny card reading, 'For you, Maria.'

By the day of the christening Trevor had already completed miniatures of paintings by Monet, Albers, Rembrandt, Ingres, Allston, Neel, Israels, Constable, Hockney, O'Keeffe and Lancret. He had just three to go – actually two and a half, for he was already halfway through 'Mares and Foals' by the English eighteenth-century painter George Stokes. Trevor had hoped that Maria would recognise his work and seek him out. The truth was she *had* been searching, going from student to student during classes in an effort to recognise the artist's hand, but never once did she look over Trevor's shoulder.

Trevor was brought out of his day-dreaming by a large slap on the back from a very drunk Dermot.

'There yeh are, Trevor, great crack isn't it?' Dermot was dribbling at this stage. By Dermot's side, as if stitched to his hip, stood Buster Brady – he too was three sheets to the wind. Dermot opened his arms wide to hug Trevor – always when Dermot had a few drinks he liked to hug everybody, especially his brothers.

From across the room Agnes watched her two sons hug, and she smiled. Pierre also saw the boys and glanced at Agnes's happy face.

'You are happy, Agnes, yes?' he asked.

'Sure, why wouldn't I be, with all me family here together in one room?' She took a mouthful from her glass of cider, and smiled again.

Little did Agnes Browne know that this night would be the last time she would see her entire family together. For fate and tragic coincidence were about to take a hand and scatter her brood to the four winds.

Chapter 3

WHEN AGNES BROWNE AND HER SIX CHILDREN had moved in next door to the Brady family on Wolfe Tone Grove, Dermot, then fourteen, had befriended the only boy of the Brady family – Buster, also fourteen. The friendship was immediate and rock solid. They had little in common, certainly not in looks. Dermot was lean, blond and handsome. Buster was short, stubby, overweight, with a red face that seemed to smile all the time. But what they did have in common was a love of practical jokes, pranks, and petty crimes.

The suburb of Finglas was divided into two halves, west and east. The dividing line was a river, a tributary of the Tolka river, known locally only as 'The River'. The two youngsters spent their early days together roaming the fields and exploring the banks of the river.

It was Buster who noticed it first. Dermot was lying beneath a giant chestnut tree set in about twenty feet from the river bank, and Buster was standing down on the edge of the bank skimming stones along the river when he called out.

Dermo! Look!'

'What is it?' Dermot answered, half asleep.

'A hole,' Buster exclaimed.

'It's probably a fox's hole.'

'How would yeh know?'

'Well, has it got a fox's tail over it?'

It took just a little time before Buster burst into hysterical laughter as he did every time Dermot made a funny comment. Then Buster searched along the river bank for a large stick and began to dig out the hole in the bank. From where Dermot sat all he could see was Buster's head bobbing up and down and clay flying in all directions. Suddenly all activity stopped.

Dermot sat up. 'Are yeh all right, Buster?' he called.

There was no reply. Dermot got up and went to the edge of the river bank. Buster had vanished.

'Buster! Hey, Buster!' Dermot was concerned now.

Then Buster's red face appeared below him, sticking out of the bank like a big-game hunter's trophy.

'It's huge, Dermo,' he announced, beaming.

Within seconds Dermot had scrambled down the bank, climbed through Buster's now excavated hole and found himself in a cavern. It was huge. It was very nearly square. What Dermot found weird was that it looked man-made. The four walls were made of rough-hewn rocks carefully placed upon each other and the roof was heavy timber beams butted together. The entrance Buster had dug out was in fact a doorway. The two boys sat in wonderment – this was indeed a magical discovery for two fourteen-year-olds. Their imaginations ran wild.

Dermot suggested it might be a hermit's home. Buster asked, 'Like Herman's Hermits?' Dermot didn't reply, he just gave Buster one of 'those' looks.

Buster then suggested that as it was so close to the Casino cinema maybe it was where Butch Cassidy and the Sundance Kid used to hide.

Dermot's look didn't change. Buster shut up.

'This is great!' Dermot half-whispered as he looked around. 'Yeh, this is really great. This'll be our headquarters, Buster, the headquarters of the Boot Hill Gang.'

The idea of the Boot Hill Gang had been to recruit as many ne'er-do-wells as possible to serve under Dermot and start a real crime ring. Recruitment wasn't going well, and after ten days the Boot Hill Gang still sported only two members.

Over the next few days the boys moved bits of furniture into the cavern and stored twelve dozen wax candles there, courtesy of the local hardware shop, although the local hardware shop owners were unaware that they had made such a donation. They even had a primus stove, which they used to cook tins of beans. The very first tin of beans they heated up on this primus stove exploded just as Buster was asking, 'How will we open the tin, Dermo?'

They kept the place a secret from everyone – everyone, that is, except Dermot's mother Agnes Browne. She insisted on knowing where Dermot and Buster were going day after day. So, reluctantly, Dermot took her down to see their new-found den, fully expecting that she would make them close it up and never play there again. Instead, Agnes was charmed by the whole thing and indeed complimented the boys on how good a job they had done in furnishing the place. She was afraid to ask where the candles had come from.

To Buster it was just a great place to play, but to Dermot it seemed more than that. There was something about the place; he wasn't sure what it was. At night from his bedroom window he would look across the field and see the chestnut tree silhouetted against the dark blue sky and his heart would lift. There was a special kind of magic about the place. That summer of 1970, Buster and Dermot filled the place with the booty of their shoplifting forays.

On some nights Agnes would let Dermot stay over and he would spend those nights making up stories to tell Buster about knights in shining armour, and about ancient heroes like Brian Boru and Cúchulainn. Buster would sit with his chin resting on his knees, marvelling at each word that came out of Dermot's mouth. They christened the place 'Chestnut Hole'.

*   *   *

In truth, Dermot and Buster were probably the two most unsuccessful criminals in Ireland. They ran all of their operations strictly in accordance with Murphy's Law – anything that could go wrong usually did.

For instance Buster once had a brainwave that they should run a street raffle. The idea was that he and Dermot would buy a book of cloakroom tickets and they would go door-to-door, street by street, selling the tickets for tenpence each, and offering a prize of five pounds to the winner. The scam was that there would actually be no winner. They would simply tell the residents of Wolfe Tone Park that somebody on Wolfe Tone Grove had won the prize, and they would tell the residents of Wolfe Tone Grove that somebody on Wolfe Tone Park had won it – and they would keep the ten pounds for the Boot Hill Gang.

Sales began well, with one customer for every three calls. When asked what cause the raffle was for, Buster would simply say 'Silver Circle'. Every school at that time had a Silver Circle raffle to raise funds for sports and such things. Within a couple of hours, ninety-nine tickets for the raffle were sold and the nine pounds ninety pence, nearly all of it in coins, had Dermot Browne's trousers nearly falling around his ankles. They made six more calls in an effort to sell the last ticket, number 100, and after leaving the sixth door Dermot finally said, 'Ah, nine pound ninety is enough, come on, we'll call it a day.'

But Buster, now full of enthusiasm that his scam was working out, insisted on carrying on. 'Just one more call, Dermo, just one more – come on, we'll try this one here.'

The house he had picked was No. 57 Wolfe Tone Park. It had an overgrown garden that looked like a jungle. Someone had once taken the trouble of planting a privet hedge right around the garden, but it obviously hadn't been cut for many years and was now as high as one of the fences in the Aintree Grand National. Dusk was falling and as the two boys walked up the path the garden seemed gloomy. The front door had once been painted buttercup yellow, but now the paint was faded, cracked and peeling. The solid brass door handle and knocker were the same as those on every house in Wolfe Tone Park and Grove – they were usually polished with pride by most of the housewives, but here they were dull to the point of being nearly black.

The two boys arrived on the doorstep and Buster rattled the knocker. For a few moments there was no sound, and Dermot, with a nudge to Buster and a nod of his head, indicated that they should leave. Just as they were about to turn away they heard the sound of a chair being dragged across a floor to the door. Through the bubbled glass windows of the side panels of the doorway they could see a tiny figure climbing up on the chair, and then they heard the clank of a bolt as it was pulled back. The tiny figure climbed down again and the boys could hear the sound of the chair being pulled back from the door. Another clank indicated that the bottom bolt was now being pulled back and after a little fumbling at the Yale lock the door creaked open. The tiny elderly woman that peered through the crack in the door had more lines on her face than you'd find on an AA road map. She had two tiny little grey eyes, no eyebrows that the boys could see and frizzy hair that seemed to grow in patches on her head. Buster later remarked that she looked a hundred and fifty years old. She wasn't. She was ninety-three. Her name was Nan Sheridan, and she had been moved out to 57 Wolfe Tone Park five years previously from her tenement in Frederick Street.

Nan had met and married Robert Sheridan in 1903, and she soon gave birth to two sons, both of whom she reared with great care. Shortly after her second boy was born her husband Robert died in Blanchardstown Hospital of tuberculosis. So, over the next few years, Nan held down four to five cleaning jobs per day and used the money to educate her two boys. The two boys, Nan would proudly tell anyone who would listen, went on to become a solicitor and a doctor. They both married beautiful girls and Nan remembers the wedding days as being two of the best days of her life. By the time Nan Sheridan was faced that night with the Boot Hill Gang at her front door, however, she hadn't seen either of her sons for four years.

'D'yeh want to buy a raffle ticket, missus?' Buster asked in his polished sales tone.

'A raffle ticket? For what?'

'For the Silver Circle.'

'And what would I do with a Silver Circle?'

'No, it's for five pounds,' Buster tried to explain.

'Five pounds a ticket! Jesus Christ, that's very dear.'

Dermot could see that this wasn't going too well, so he interjected in an effort to straighten things out.

'Look, missus, the tickets are tenpence each. The prize is five pounds. The money is going to the Silver Circle. Now, d'yeh want one or not?'

'Ten pence, now that's different. That's very reasonable. Come in, boys.'

The two boys entered the house and Nan Sheridan ushered them through the hallway into the front room. Apart from the three bodies that had just entered it, the front room contained just two armchairs and a china cabinet. On top of the china cabinet were two wedding photographs.

'Wait here now, boys, and I'll get you the ten pence,' Nan said, and she vanished into the kitchen.

'Holy fuck!' Dermot exclaimed. He was looking up at the ceiling, where a bare bulb hung from the cable. 'She has nothing.'

Nan soon emerged from the kitchen, opened her hand and into Buster's palm she dropped seven pence. The two boys looked at the four brown coins.

'There's seven pence and I have three pence upstairs I think, hold on.' She turned to leave the room.

'Hold it, missus,' Dermot tried to stop her, 'seven pence will do. You're all right, we'll let yeh off with the three pence.'

'No, no, I wouldn't hear of it! That wouldn't be fair to all the other people who bought tickets. I don't know why I'm doing this, I never won anything in me life,' the old woman moaned good-heartedly.

Listening to the sound of Nan painfully making her way up the stairs the two boys from the Boot Hill Gang felt very small. It was five minutes before she returned with the three pence, smiling she handed it over to Dermot. Dermot tore out ticket No. 100 and placed it in Nan Sheridan's wrinkled palm. She walked to the china cabinet and put the ticket carefully under the frame of one of the wedding photographs.

'It'll be safe here. Right, boys, let me show you out.'

The two boys left and began to make their way home to Wolfe Tone Grove. At first neither of them spoke. Eventually when conversation did start it was stilted.

'Good scam, eh?' Dermot said.

'Eh ... yeh.' Buster sounded decidedly unenthusiastic.

'Ten pounds – it's not to be sneezed at. We could do this every week and get away with it!'

'Yeh, Dermo, great isn't it?'

'I feel bleedin' terrible,' Dermot announced eventually, and he stopped and leaned against somebody's railings.

'So do I, Dermo, I feel shite.'

They both knew what had to be done. So they did it.

* * *

'I couldn't believe me luck,' Nan Sheridan told the girl in the post office next day. 'Honestly, I thought they said five pounds of a prize, but I got a hamper *and* five pounds. And d'yeh know, I never won anything before in me life!' She was smiling happily as she pushed her pension book across the counter to the young postmistress along with the five-pound note that she had been given as the prize by Dermot and Buster.

The young girl stamped the woman's pension book, both on the voucher and on the stub, tore out the voucher and began to count out the eight pounds seventy-five pence cash. She passed the cash across to the woman along with the turf voucher she was entitled to. She then picked up the five-pound note and asked Nan Sheridan, 'What d'yeh want for this again, love?'

Nan began to explain. 'I want two postal orders, both for two pounds fifty. One made out to Liam Sheridan and the other made out to Philip Sheridan. They're me sons, and they haven't had time to get out and see me recently, so I thought with me winnings I'd send them the price of a drink – well, yeh know the way it is with boys, yeh have to look after them.'

The Boot Hill Gang's first scam had cost them forty pence.

* * *

Having said all that, the Boot Hill Gang did have some minor successes as would become evident if one had the opportunity to browse through the contents of Chestnut Hole. It contained toasters, electric kettles, small pieces of silver jewellery, and, thanks to Buster's learning difficulties, two large brown cardboard cases of what were supposed to be transistor radios but were actually toilet rolls. Chestnut Hole, having served the two boys well as a play house in their teens, now served them in their mid-twenties as an excellent store-room. This is exactly what Dermot Browne was thinking as he pushed the large boxes of bum rolls aside to get at his 'hidey hole' – a loose brick in the south wall of Chestnut Hole, behind which Dermot kept his own little valuables (things like the condoms he had bought on a trip to Northern Ireland once, or about two hundred pounds he liked to have in case of an emergency). He also used his 'hidey hole' for his stash of cannabis. Dermot had got onto the dope soon after meeting up with Mary Carter. After a couple of unsuccessful attempts, Dermot eventually got his first 'hit' and now relished the thought of a 'bit of blow' before introducing his 'soldier of fortune' to a most welcoming Mary Carter. It was the 'blow' that Dermot removed from his hidey hole this night. After sticking the two little five-spot packs into the breast pocket of his mohair suit, Dermot checked his hair in the small mirror just beside the entrance of Chestnut Hole, straightened his tie and set off for another night of passion with Mary. Although Dermot Browne hadn't found a love life yet, his sex life was doing fine.

Chapter 4

'THIS CAN BE A WONDERFUL TIME OF LIFE –' Pierre began.

'Shut up, Pierre,' Agnes snapped. Agnes didn't like Pierre talking when she was thinking.

There were four people sitting in the kitchen of Agnes Browne's home in Wolfe Tone Grove. Along with herself and her beau Pierre, on the far side of the kitchen table sat Agnes's daughter Cathy and her own beau, Garda Mick O'Leary. For a few moments there was silence. Then Mick coughed, one of those coughs that you know is going to be followed by a sentence.

'It's the way my work is, Mrs Browne. Guards get transferred all the time. I suppose I'm just lucky that it's Wicklow and not Donegal, somewhere real far away.'

'That's exactly me point, son. Just because you're getting transferred is not a good enough excuse for the two of you to get married. I mean, where will you live down there?'

Mick and Cathy looked at each other as if both were going to speak. Mick leaned back, allowing Cathy to go on.

'Mick has found a beautiful mobile home at the back of a cottage that we can rent. It's near Brittas Bay, Mammy, just a few hundred yards from the beach!' Cathy's voice was excited.

'Ah yes. Mobile homes today are a lot more comfortable than they used –' Pierre began.

'Shut up, Pierre,' Agnes said again. Agnes had no objection to what was being said. She didn't mind the idea of her daughter moving away from Dublin to live with the man she loved. She didn't even mind that they would start their married life in a caravan; in fact she thought that quite charming. But there was something niggling at her. It was Mick O'Leary – she couldn't put her finger on it but there was something about him. At first she had liked him a lot and was happy that her daughter had found a man she loved, but the more she came to know Mick the more concerned she got. There definitely was something about him that unsettled her. Her own mother used to describe it as his 'gimp'. That was it, there was a peculiar gimp about him. These days 'gimp' would probably be translated as 'karma'. Mick O'Leary had bad karma.

Agnes stood up from the table. 'I need a cigarette,' she announced. She left to go into the front room where her handbag was. Pierre followed. When the couples were separated by a wall, two different conversations took place. In the kitchen Cathy looked dolefully at Mick and asked, 'Well, what d'yeh think?'

'Well, I'm prepared to go along with this sham so far, Cathy, but I'll tell yeh, you're old enough to know your own mind and I don't give a fuck what she says, we're getting married.'

'I know we will, Mick, but wouldn't it be better if she was in favour of it and there would be no hassles then?' Cathy pleaded.

'Yeh, I suppose so.' Mick crossed his arms and stared at the ceiling.

In the other room Agnes was rooting in her handbag for her cigarettes, and Pierre came up behind her.

'Why do you ask me to sit in on these family conversations?'

'For mortal support,' Agnes answered with a cigarette between her lips, scratching a match on the side of a box.

'But you won't let me speak.'

'Mortal support doesn't include speakin',' Agnes said matter-of-factly, and made her way towards the door.

Before she got there Pierre said, 'I think they *should* marry!'

Agnes stopped in her tracks and slowly turned. She took the cigarette from her lips and exhaled the smoke slowly.

'Do yeh now, Pierre, and why d'yeh think they should marry?' Agnes asked him.

'Because they want to.'

'I see, because they want to! And if Cathy decided to pour petrol over herself and put a match to it, would that be all right, if she *wanted to*?'

'Don't be ridiculous, that's not what I mean. They are in love.'

'Love, me arse! For a marriage to work it needs a lot more than *just* love.'

'Agnes, you sound like a woman that has never been loved.'

'And, Pierre, you sound like a man that has never been fuckin' married.'

With that Agnes turned on her heel and re-entered the kitchen. After a few moments' pause for thought, Pierre did likewise. He took his seat by Agnes's side and Agnes began to speak to the couple.

'Well, I don't have to tell the two of you that marriage is a huge step. You're both adults and if your minds are set on it I'll not stand in your way. I'll just ask you this, to be kind to each other and remember how together you feel right at this moment, because it's only that togetherness that will make your marriage work. Love will make your marriage happy, but first you need to make your marriage work.'

The young couple smiled and hugged each other, then Mick stood up, walked around the table and kissed Agnes – and got quite a surprise when Pierre leaned over and kissed him. After a couple of cups of tea the wedding date was set for the twenty-fourth of August, and preliminary wedding lists were drawn up.

News of the impending marriage was received with mixed reactions in the Browne household. Mark and Betty were delighted for the couple and Mark immediately promised them a wedding present of a suite of furniture. Rory and Dino both wanted to go to Hickey's fabric shop with Cathy to help pick out her wedding dress and bridesmaids' fabrics. Dermot and Buster Brady threw up – a Garda in the Browne family was unthinkable. Simon and his girlfriend Fiona Rock were delighted for the couple and Fiona was doubly delighted when Cathy, having no sisters, asked Fiona to be her maid of honour. Trevor Browne's heart sank when he heard the news. Not that he was disappointed for Mick and Cathy – quite the opposite, he was delighted to see Cathy so happy. His heart sank because he wished it was *him* announcing the news that he was about to marry Maria Nicholson.

Trevor's plan was not going well. He now had just one painting to complete, a beautiful piece by Nicholson, fittingly called 'Relief'. Yet Maria Nicholson herself was no nearer to finding the mysterious artist and Trevor no closer to declaring his love for her. But he had made one giant leap forward. On two mornings in succession while passing her in the corridor he had said, 'Good morning, Maria.' But her replies were disappointing. On the first morning she answered, 'Good morning, Terry,' and on the second she didn't even venture a name, she just said, 'Yes it is, isn't it?' On the evening when he completed the Nicholson piece Trevor sat in his bedroom putting the final touches to the tiny frame when Rory entered the room wearing one strawberry pink sock and in search of the other.

'Trevor, yeh didn't notice a sock lying around, did yeh?'

'No, and if it's the match for that one you're wearing I'm sure I would have.'

'Very funny. I like bright colours, okay?' Rory suddenly noticed the tiny painting in Trevor's hand. 'Jesus, Trevor, that's beautiful. How much will it sell for?'

Trevor chuckled and told Rory that this painting wasn't for sale – and he went on to explain to Rory that a true artist didn't create his paintings for sale anyway, he painted them because he had to. This is why so many painters died penniless.

'Well, if you're not goin' to sell it, what are yeh goin' to do with it?'

'I'm going to give it to someone.'

'Who?'

'A friend of mine.'

'A friend? Oh, *a friend!* Who is she?' Rory sat down opposite Trevor on the bed ready to be filled with gossip.

'Ah, it's a long story, Rory. It doesn't really matter.' Trevor tried to brush Rory off, but Rory wasn't having any of it.

'It must matter if you're doin' a paintin' like that. It is a girl, isn't it?'

Trevor looked into Rory's face and two things struck him. Firstly, Rory was genuinely delighted that it might be a girl, and secondly, Rory wasn't surprised that Trevor might have a girlfriend. Rory's confidence in his female pulling power relaxed Trevor and for the first time he told somebody else the entire story of Maria Nicholson, the pictures and his failure to get a response. Rory sat silently throughout the whole story, although changing his expression at every twist and turn in the plot. By the time Trevor had finished, Rory sat, his circular glasses sliding down his nose and his mouth agape. Trevor indicated the end of the story with a shrug of his shoulders.

Rory almost attacked him. 'Jaysus, Trevor, yeh have to tell her!'

'I can't! I just can't.'

'Yeh have to. Jesus, Trevor, that's beautiful, I nearly feel like riding yeh meself!' The two young men laughed, but as soon as the laughter died down Rory returned to the attack.

'I'm serious, Trevor, you have to take that girl – Maria is it? – you have to take her aside and tell her how you feel. I can't tell you how many of my gay friends, before they came out, were in love with people and didn't tell them and every single one of them regrets it to this day. Some of them are still depressed about it years later. For God's sake don't let this chance go by.'

'So what do I do, Rory? I just walk up and say I love yeh?'

Rory thought for a moment. 'No, Trevor. After all you've done so far all you have to do is give her this picture yourself! Yeh don't have to say anythin'. Yeh don't have to tell her yeh love her, just walk up to her and give her this last picture yourself. I swear to God, Trevor, that'll do the job. If it doesn't she's a hard-hearted bitch and you're better off without her anyway.' Again the two men laughed.

'I'll do it,' Trevor announced. 'I will, I'll walk up to her and I'll give her the picture. Jesus, thanks Rory, that's all I needed, yeh know, somebody to tell me that I have to do it. And I do, I have to do it.'

The two brothers hugged each other, and Trevor looked forward to the following day. He slept well and dreamed about handing his picture to the beautiful Maria Nicholson. The next day was Friday and Trevor shared the bus into town with Dermot and Buster who were both going to collect their dole money from the unemployment exchange.

Chapter 5

THE THIRTEEN TINY FRAMED WORKS OF ART stood in a row right across the top of the polished grand piano. The initial letter of each name on the copies spelt out M–A–R–I–A N–I–C–H–O–L–S–O–. Maria sat on the arm of the couch engrossed in the parade of tiny masterpieces. She held her mug of scalding tea in her cupped hands and every now and then she took a sip without taking her eyes from the pictures. When Maria's mother Edith had buttered and applied marmalade to the toast, she made her way to the drawing room where she knew her daughter would be. She also knew exactly what she would be doing. She came to Maria's side and handed her the plate. She too looked at the miniature paintings.

'You're due an "N" any day now, aren't you, honey?' Edith asked her daughter.

Maria nodded several times before speaking. 'Yes.'

'Still no idea who it is?'

Maria snapped out of her trance at her mother's second question.

'No, not a clue, Mum. I've looked at virtually everybody's work and nothing compares to these. I've also studied all the likely candidates and none of them, that I can tell, would have the depth of feeling that it took to even conceive this,' she swept her hand across the room indicating the pictures, 'let alone to sit down and paint them. But he's in that college somewhere.'

Edith took the plate and mug from her daughter and, pointing to the clock, exclaimed, 'And so should you be, Miss, go on, off you go.'

Maria put on her coat while her mother watched her fondly. 'Maybe he'll be here at the party tomorrow night?'

Maria spun around and giggled. 'Isn't it just like Cinderella, Mum?'

Edith gave her daughter a hug. 'Darling, when you're young every love affair should make you feel like Cinderella.'

*   *   *

The tiny painting was burning a hole in Trevor's pocket. Every minute that he did not see Maria Nicholson, the little picture felt heavier, and he became more terrified. The psychological weight of the picture became so great that Trevor even began to limp, as if he were carrying a huge object in his pocket.

He had hoped to catch her eye in the corridor some time between the first two classes. The first two attempts didn't go well. After the first class she was nowhere to be seen. After his second class he saw her but as he made his way towards her she slipped up a couple of flights of stairs to a classroom. Eventually lunchtime came and Trevor made his way down to the canteen where he knew for sure Maria Nicholson would be dining. Entering the canteen he saw her sitting at a table with six other girls. He very nearly walked straight over and placed the picture down in front of her, but instinct told him to wait, and instead he went to the self-service counter where he got himself a mug of coffee and a chocolate éclair. He paid for his goodies and made his way to a table where he sat with a few guys who shared some classes with him. All of the time his eyes were on Maria Nicholson. One of the boys noticed his stare and nudged him.

'Nice, isn't she?' he said.

'What? Eh yeh, I suppose, yeh she is – beautiful.' Trevor blushed.

'Where are we all going to meet before the party?' one of the others enquired.

'What party?' Trevor asked.

It was Noel King who answered. 'Tomorrow night, at Maria Nicholson's house. Her party, didn't you get an invitation?'

Trevor quietly answered, 'No.'

''Of course, you only have two classes a week with her! She probably doesn't even know you. She's invited all the lads. Come on, I'll introduce you,' Noel stood up.

Trevor panicked. 'No, no, I'm grand – no, you're all right – I *have* met her, no, it's okay, thanks.' He got up from the table and hurried out of the canteen, leaving half a cup of coffee and an untouched chocolate éclair.

*　　*　　*

'I can't just gate-crash somebody's party!' Trevor threw his arms in the air in frustration and walked away from Dino and Rory who were sitting in two empty stylist's chairs in an empty Wash & Blow hairdressing salon. The shop had been closed for an hour.

'*I* would!' Dino Doyle exclaimed.

Trevor spun round. 'Well of course *you* would. You don't give a shite what people think about yeh – oh I don't mean that in the wrong way, Dino. Yeh know what I mean, you've got lots of confidence.'

'I'm not takin' it the wrong way, Trevor. I *don't* give a shite what people think about me. But that's not the point here. I guarantee you that if this girl knew that you were the one that had painted those pictures you would be top of the invitation list. Am I right, Rory?'

'You're dead right, Dino. He's right, Trevor. Yeh have to gate-crash the party.'

Rory and Dino stared at Trevor. After a few moments hesitation, Trevor dug his hands into his pockets and asked, 'Okay, so how do I do it?'

Rory and Dino were delighted, and Rory squealed, 'Oooh, come on, Dino, let's make a plan!'

The plan, as it turned out, was very simple. Trevor would simply arrive the following night at the Nicholson house on Belgrave Square. He would knock at the door while the party was in full swing. Whoever opened the door would simply accept that he was one of the students and allow him in. Immediately on entering, Dino and Rory insisted, Trevor was to find Maria Nicholson, no matter where she was, walk straight up to her, hand her the unwrapped picture, and say, 'Add this to your collection, Maria.'

Dino and Rory made Trevor rehearse it in the mirror. At first he sounded like John Wayne trying to feign a tough-guy image. Rory and Dino said that although they found it attractive they thought it a little shallow. After a few more attempts Trevor eventually sounded like Trevor, and Rory and Dino were satisfied.

Saturday-morning breakfast in the Browne house was always a big attraction. It was the morning when Mammy cooked her famous fry. Each member of the family would sit down to a red-hot plate of black pudding, white pudding, grilled tomatoes, mushrooms, Haffner's sausages, and narrow back rashers. They would have a choice of toast or fried bread and copious amounts of scalding hot, strong leaf tea – none of that tea-bag stuff for our Agnes.

Now, Rory Browne was a great brother. He was also a wonderful friend and lover, as Dino could testify. But he had one flaw, and it was his mother who always pointed it out: Rory couldn't 'hold his piss'. This was Agnes's euphemism for not being able to keep a secret. Trevor nearly died of embarrassment when Rory announced, 'Tonight's a big night for our Trevor!'

Knives were slowly put down. Mugs were settled and one or two cigarettes were lit up in the silence that followed Rory's announcement. Agnes was the one who asked the question on everybody's lips: 'Why, what's on tonight, Trevor?'

Trevor's face turned so red it seemed he was fit to burst. Grinding his teeth together, he mumbled the words, 'Fuck yeh, Rory.' Rory, sensing Trevor's inability to explain to the family what the big occasion was, took it upon himself to fill the entire family in on the state of Trevor's love affair or, as he would point out, non-love affair. Everyone was delighted for Trevor and there were various pats on the back or little thumps from well-wishing brothers, and a hug and a kiss from Cathy. Trevor was embarrassed by all this at first, but actually took some strength from the support offered by his family and now relished the thought of delivering into Maria Nicholson's hand the last of his works of art.

That day dragged on for Trevor. Every minute seemed to last an eternity, but eventually eight o'clock came and, dressed in his newest black Levi's, a grandfather shirt, and black leather jacket, Trevor looked every inch the cool art-college student. Rory and Dermot gave their approval, and Trevor headed for Maria Nicholson's party.

Belgrave Square was beautiful, an expansive square of Victorian houses which surrounded a railed recreation area known as the Parish Priest's Park. There were five entrances into the park, one midway along each row of railings at opposite sides of the park and one on the corner that faced the city centre. Trevor stood half-hidden by a bush inside the gateway on the western side of the square. He was now across the street and three houses away from Maria Nicholson's home. From where he stood he could hear the rhythmic beat of Desmond Decker hammering out 'The Israelites', a song Trevor always loved but never understood a word of. Every so often a car would drive up, a young man or a young woman

45

would get out and go in to the party. He recognised most of them. From where he stood in the gateway he was about two hundred yards from a green postbox on the same side of the road. This post box was two houses past Maria's house. He had walked to and from the postbox ten times so far, all of the time mumbling to himself, 'Add this to your collection.'

Trevor's shirt collar button was now open and he was sweating. His hands were dug deep into his pockets and he shuffled his feet. Suddenly he said aloud, 'I can't do it,' and walked away. As he rounded the corner from Belgrave Square into Victoria Street he came upon a lighted 'phone box. He went in and dialled his mother's number. Rory answered.

'Rory? It's me, Trevor.'

'Trevor? Well, how's the party goin'?'

'It's goin' great, the music is brilliant.'

'What's the food like?'

'Eh ... I don't know, I don't know.'

'Did yeh not eat any?'

There was now a pause during which Rory twigged.

'Ah Trevor, don't tell me yeh didn't fuckin' go in?'

'I can't do it, Rory.'

''Course yeh can, Trevor, yeh have to!'

'But ... but I seen loads of people go in, Rory, I know them all – what if she starts laughing?'

'Trevor Browne, I don't know where that 'phone box you're in is, but you get your arse back to that door now and you go in and give that girl that paintin' or I swear I'll never talk to yeh again. I mean it!'

It was Rory who terminated the call. Trevor stood for a couple of moments with the whining earpiece against his ear. Slowly he replaced the handset, left the 'phone box and began to stroll. Before he realised it he was standing at the bottom of steps outside Maria Nicholson's house. He took his hands from his pockets, closed his shirt button, stuck his chin out and, murmuring 'Ah fuck it' made his way up the steps and rapped on the door. The man who opened it was about six inches taller then Trevor. He was wearing a white shirt and white bow tie, over which he wore a red coat of tails. Ever so grandly the man said, 'Good evening, sir, may I see your invitation please?'

* * *

Rory, Dino, Dermot and Agnes were sitting around the kitchen table having their late night cup of tea and a chat when they heard the front door opening. Agnes looked up at the kitchen clock, it was two thirty in the morning. Rory smiled and winked at her. All four were looking at the doorway long before Trevor's frame filled it. He was drunk, very drunk. His hair was tossed, there was a brownish dribble coming down the right-hand side of his mouth and his eyes were glazed. Everybody wanted to, but nobody dared ask the question. Trevor took four unsteady steps to the kitchen table. He plunged his hand into his jacket pocket and withdrew the tiny little painting. The eyes of all four at the table were riveted on it. Trevor simply tossed it on the table, turned and went to bed. Nobody said a word. No words were necessary.

Trevor Browne's usual routine on a Sunday morning was to have an early-morning breakfast, after which he would pack his bag with his sketch pad and pencils and bus his way to some locale where he would sketch for most of the day. Even after the previous night's events this Sunday was to be no different, except this Sunday he had his breakfast in silence. As Agnes went to pour him his second cup of tea, Trevor simply held his hand up indicating that he wasn't about to have one. Instead he stood up, took his plate, cup and saucer, one on top of the other, to the sink and placed them on the draining board. Agnes picked up the tiny painting off the kitchen window ledge where she had put it and handed it to Trevor without a word. Trevor looked at the painting and then looked at his mother's face. He smiled and said, 'I don't want it, Mammy, you keep it!' Then he left for his day's sketching.

Agnes was disappointed and upset for her son and her heart was heavy for most of the day. However, it lightened as tea time came, for she had arranged to go to Mark and Betty's for tea, after which Mark and Betty were going out and Agnes would have baby Aaron all to herself. He was such a good child, a real joy to look after. When Mark and Betty had dressed and left to meet their friends, Agnes cleaned up the kitchen and tidied around the sitting room a little. She then heated Aaron's bottle to body tempera-ture, fed him and changed his nappy, but instead of putting him back down in his cot she turned on the Sunday night movie and lay on the couch with baby Aaron lying on her chest. She looked down at the tiny little face, his eyes fluttering now and then. Nothing, she thought, could replace the sweet smell of a baby's breath as it slept.

Mark and Betty returned at a respectable hour and the car was still nice and warm when Agnes got into it for the journey home. It had been a lovely evening for Agnes, quiet and peaceful and in the company of her grandson, so lovely in fact that by the time she rose the next morning she had almost forgotten about Trevor's disappointment. Almost, that is, until she saw the picture on the window ledge as she was putting the kettle on.

Her sadness was short-lived. Trevor entered the kitchen with determination in his walk. He made his way straight to the kitchen sink and plucked the painting from the ledge. Agnes stared into his face. There was a fire in his eyes and his chin was set in grim determination. Trevor simply said, 'Maria Nicholson is getting this picture whether she fuckin' likes it or not, Mammy,' and he left the house.

By tea time that evening Agnes had related Trevor's entrance and exit to the entire family. They sat at the tea table awaiting his return. Dermot had even forgone a date with Mary Carter in anticipation of the celebrations to come. They all knew as soon as he entered that whatever had happened that day it wasn't what Trevor had expected to happen. Trevor sat at the only empty chair around the table and, as his mother poured him out a cup of tea, he said, 'Before any of you ask, no, I didn't give the picture to Maria Nicholson, but wait, it's not because I didn't want to or I wasn't goin' to –' Trevor began to tell them the story.

It hadn't even dawned on Trevor to wonder why Maria Nicholson should be having a party. Was it her birthday? He didn't know – he didn't want to know, because all that was on his mind on that Saturday evening was how he was going to give her his picture. When he got to college that Monday he went from classroom to classroom looking for Maria Nicholson. He didn't find her and when he enquired at the reception desk they said they hadn't seen her come in that morning. It was Noel King who told him what the story was. Maria's father had received a contract from an Irish-based company, but to do a job on a bridge in New Zealand. The party was a going-away party. After college that day Trevor made his way to Belgrave Square. The house was empty. Maria Nicholson was gone.

The family listened to Trevor's story in complete silence. Trevor hadn't told it in a frustrated manner, nor in an angry manner, he told it in a manner which made you believe that this is what he had expected to happen. When he had finished his story and his tea, Trevor went to his own bedroom. He removed the frame from the picture, and carefully took the staples from the canvas. He then placed the tiny canvas flat in his wallet, where it would remain to remind him that if love ever came knocking on his door again he should indeed grasp it with both hands.

Chapter 6

AGNES BROWNE'S SIX LIVING CHILDREN were now all adults. It seems incredible that in their adulthood five of the six should still be living at home. However, this is not unusual for an Irish mother. Agnes didn't complain; the fact was, she loved it. She would gladly have allowed them to stay forever. She had always known that Mark would be the first to marry and leave the nest, but she hadn't expected that Cathy's marriage would begin the exodus it did.

The marriage ceremony of Cathy Browne to Mick O'Leary took place in St Canice's Church in Finglas village on the twenty-fourth of August, Cathy's twenty-third birthday. The O'Leary family travelled up from Bishopstown in Cork, and within hours of arriving in Dublin, felt like they had known the Browne family all their lives. Mick's father Thomas, a former policeman himself, eyed Dermot and Buster suspiciously, but other than that settled in well. Agnes didn't really take to him. He was a very rigid man. He always spoke very loudly, unlike his wife Florie, who seemed quiet and retiring. The only boy of the O'Leary household, Mick had four sisters, all of whom could be recognised by their one common physical feature, a mouthful of teeth so crooked they looked like badly kept graveyards. Dermot christened them 'Gums and Bullets'.

There seemed to be little affection between father and son in the O'Leary family. Agnes noticed that Mr O'Leary always spoke to Mick in a military fashion. She had remarked on this to Winnie the Mackerel one day, standing in the Moore Street sunshine, after her first visit to the O'Learys in Cork. 'He offered me a cup of tea,' she told Winnie, 'and I felt like fuckin' saluting him.'

On the other hand, Agnes had hit it off really well with Florie O'Leary. In looks, she reminded Agnes of her late friend Marion Monks.

The ceremony went really well. Cathy arrived at the church accompanied by Pierre, her surrogate father, who proudly marched her down the aisle. Agnes was in tears. Mrs Browne's boys stood with their chests puffed out, immensely proud of this vision of beauty that was their sister. The wedding reception was held in Barry's Hotel, on Gardiner Row in Dublin's city centre. The food was piping hot and there was plenty of it, and the music was provided by Billy Hughes, who lashed out the Tom Jones

51

numbers one after the other. It was a wonderful evening and all of the guests without exception had a fabulous time. Cathy would always remember one small incident from the entire day. At the appropriate time during the reception party she and her new husband left to change into their going-away clothes. When they returned to the reception room to be greeted by both families, there were hugs and kisses all round. As Florie O'Leary put her arms around Cathy to say farewell, she whispered in her ear, 'Remember this, dear, don't lie down, whatever you do don't lie down.' Cathy hadn't a clue what Florie O'Leary had meant, but she would soon learn.

The 'happy couple' were still on honeymoon when two more of the Browne boys announced their intention of leaving the nest. Dino Doyle, Rory's friend, had found an apartment, it seemed, that was very comfortable, central, but a little too expensive for him to manage alone. Rory had decided to move in with him so they could share the cost. That was the story anyway. Agnes took it at face value and didn't question Rory. Pierre often laughed to himself when he recalled one evening that he and Agnes were sitting in to watch a good movie on TV. Rory came into the room to say goodnight before heading out for the evening. He was wearing red suede shoes, red skin-tight denims, a white blouse with cravat, a studded earring in his right ear and mascara. When Rory had left the room Agnes leaned towards Pierre and whispered, 'It wouldn't surprise me a bit, Pierre, if that fella one day came out of the wardrobe – I think he's gay and doesn't know it yet!' She had completely forgotten that only two years before he had indeed 'come out of the wardrobe', but at that time Agnes didn't even understand the word 'gay'.

Agnes never voiced her suspicions to Rory or indeed ever again to Pierre. So when Rory announced his intention of moving in with Dino, Agnes feigned indifference and wished them luck. In her heart of hearts she knew what was going on, but honestly she thought it was sick, so she pretended she didn't want to know. She would never treat Dino as anything other than a stranger in her home.

More shocking even than the possibility of Rory's homosexuality was Simon's announcement. Simon had been dating Fiona Rock for some time now and Agnes always expected that they would one day marry and set up home. But she expected it to happen in that order. Instead, Simon surprised everyone by announcing that he and Fiona were to set up home before getting married. Simon explained that he and Fiona knew that they loved each other enough to want to live together. They would then see if they loved each other enough to want to marry. Mark commented that he thought it was very adult of them. Agnes on the other hand thought it was disgraceful and wasn't sure that it wasn't even illegal. Despite her reservations, Agnes had to admit two months later, after she had visited Simon and Fiona in the apartment they had taken on Rathmines Road, that they made a lovely couple and indeed their home was warm and welcoming. She and Pierre had gone over for tea and spent the evening sipping beer, or in Agnes's case cider, and chatting. Agnes remarked to Pierre on the way home that it felt like sitting in the company of friends rather than in the company of one of her sons.

On top of this, Trevor graduated from art college that September of 1980 with straight 'A's. He was immediately offered four positions from different companies in the advertising industry. Advertising was beginning to boom and good illustrators were at a premium. He eventually chose Hutchinson & Bailey as he felt they offered the biggest challenge to his talent. They were involved in the international market, which would give Trevor a chance to show his work overseas, and on top of that they offered the most money. Agnes was delighted that Trevor had been so sought after and she was full of pride in her youngest boy. She was sad, though, that he had chosen this particular company, for their head office was in Bond Street in London and it meant she was to lose yet another son – and London was a great source of pain for Agnes since Frankie had met his sad end there.

Mark drove Trevor and Agnes to the airport. Trevor sat in the front seat beside Mark and they chatted away, Mark full of compliments for his younger brother, and Trevor's voice full of excitement in anticipation of the adventure ahead of him. Agnes sat in the back seat, listening to these two men who called her Mammy, more than a little proud that they had come this far. She made the journey from Finglas to the airport in silence. She thought about Frankie and wished that she had had the chance to see him off at least.

The entrance to the departure gates at Dublin airport is fondly known to Dubliners as 'Tears and Snots'. That night was to be no exception as Agnes said goodbye to her emigrant son. When she returned to her home in Finglas Agnes stripped the linen off Trevor's bed in the boys' room, which now had four bare mattresses. She went downstairs, threw the linen into the laundry basket, went to the kitchen and took out two mugs, one for herself and one for the only other resident of 43 Wolfe Tone Grove, her son Dermot. Dermot did not return that night, so Agnes washed her mug and, for the first time that she could remember, went to bed without a late-night family chat.

Chapter 7

DURING HIS FIRST MONTH IN ENGLAND Trevor wrote a letter home every single week. The following month Agnes received just two letters, then it was down to one a month and by the time her forty-eighth birthday came, on the seventh of July 1981, Agnes would expect a letter from Trevor when she saw one. But she received a birthday card from him on that day, as she did from all of her other children and from her grandson Aaron. Aaron was soon to be joined by two more grandchildren, for Fiona had discovered just days before that she was pregnant, and Cathy was due her first child in five weeks.

There was no party for the birthday. Instead Mark and Betty had taken Agnes and Pierre out to dinner to a fancy restaurant called the Pot Pourri in Parliament Street. All of the waiters spoke French, so Pierre felt right at home. They had a lovely evening and when she returned to Wolfe Tone Grove Agnes invited Pierre to stay the night.

He readily accepted and was delighted at the thought of rattling off a couple of 'organisms'. They had a quick cup of tea and then Pierre headed up the stairs to the master bedroom. Before going up to join him, Agnes read her birthday cards again. The cards were lovely, she thought, but it's not the same as having your children around you. She spent a moment thinking about Frankie, then she climbed the stairs with a heavy heart, but brightened when she saw Pierre standing in the bedroom wearing only a pair of g-string underpants, which made him look a little like an under-nourished sumo wrestler. They made love for three and a half hours, and Agnes Browne entered her forty-ninth year a satisfied woman.

*   *   *

With just five weeks left to the due date of her first birth, Cathy was excited. She was so looking forward to being a mother. She also hoped the baby would improve things and bring her and Mick closer together. She was trying so hard to please him – she would do anything to make him happy. The trouble was, she couldn't be sure what it was that made him happy. He would tell her to dress up nicely when they were going out with his friends and their wives. He would check her over before they left, telling her to take this off and put that on. Without argument, she would always comply with his wishes, and when he was happy with how she looked they would leave for the evening. But then after a few drinks Mick would completely change and tell her she looked like a slut. Later, he would accuse her of making eyes at his friends or even at strangers in the pub. When they returned home from these evenings Mick would explode into a furious temper. The more she denied his accusations and declared her love for him and him alone, the worse he would get. She learned to stay quiet. She learned that regardless of whether she denied his accusations, or apologised, the beatings would still come. Then there would be periods when he wouldn't beat her. Instead he would call her a fool or snap at her to shut up if she began to try and make conversation.

What had happened to the man she had fallen in love with and married? Cathy became very quiet and left the house only if she had to. She liked the house, it was better than the mobile home, which had become very cold in the winter. It was a rented house in Arklow town. But it was a start, she told herself, and she kept the place spick and span. She didn't have many friends – no, the truth was she didn't have *any* friends. Mick didn't like her to have friends. He told her the townspeople weren't to be trusted and he didn't want his business to be discussed with them.

But the baby would change everything, she knew that. There would be walks on sunny days with the pram and her tiny child gurgling up at her. She prayed it would be a boy as she knew this would make Mick happy. A son to make his father proud; and she as the bearer of that son would share the glow of that pride, she hoped – no, not hoped, she was sure! Since she had become pregnant Mick had treated her with kid gloves; in fact, by his standards she was being positively spoiled, and he seemed in much better humour now, even when he was drunk. There had been a couple of drawbacks to being pregnant. For instance, Mick had decided Cathy wasn't to smoke any more, although she supposed this was a good thing. Unfortunately he had also decided that she wasn't to drink. She missed going to the pub with him and meeting other people. Still, each night he returned from the pub he brought fish and chips smothered in vinegar; she loved vinegar since she became pregnant. Yes, she was sure the baby would change everything!

*   *   *

Trevor settled in very well at Hutchinson & Bailey. Besides Trevor, there were three other artists in the creative department. They were a close-knit unit, but they welcomed Trevor in with genuine warmth. The three were Tony Vescoli, Sue White, and Bert Chadwick. It was very obvious to Trevor that Tony and Sue were 'an item'. Tony Vescoli's family came from Liverpool. They were of Italian Catholic origin and Tony had been educated in St Thomas's School for Catholic Boys in Speke before taking his art degree at Manchester University. Like Trevor, Tony had been head-hunted straight from college by Hutchinson & Bailey, albeit five years previously. Tony was a kind, likeable and even-tempered man, and he and Trevor struck up an immediate friendship.

Sue White began every day in the office like a freshly uncorked bottle of champagne. She had a smile for everybody and always seemed to see the bright side of things. Along with this ebullience, she had a motherly instinct and was the office agony aunt. She completely bowled Trevor over on his first day when she welcomed him with a huge hug, a kiss and a cup of coffee, followed by a hundred questions. She was easy to talk to and within one hour of meeting him Sue White knew more about Trevor Browne than anybody else on this planet. Sue was a natural artist and a real go-getter. She had not been head-hunted, rather she had targeted Hutchinson & Bailey in her final year at college as the company she wanted to work for. However, her interview three years previously failed to get her a position in the Bond Street office. Instead she had gone to the company's Glasgow office, with a promise of a transfer as soon as an opening came up. She jumped at the chance and was in Glasgow, where incidentally she was a huge hit, for only two years before she was brought to the head office in London. Sue was born and spent her childhood in a beautiful Tudor-style home in Camberley in Surrey not far from Ascot racecourse.

Bert Chadwick was from London's east end. A chubby man, in his mid-thirties, his only passion was soccer – to be precise, Tottenham Hotspur. His handshake, although sweaty, was firm and warm. Trevor liked him. The highlight of Bert's day was the mid-morning coffee break, where he would devour the sports pages of *The Sun* along with a half-dozen doughnuts.

Sue was deeply in love with Tony. But the problem with Sue was that she couldn't understand why everybody didn't have a love affair akin to hers and Tony's, particularly somebody as young, attractive and available as Trevor. So it became a personal challenge to her as soon as Trevor arrived in the office to match him up with a girl who would steal his heart away. This was not a first for Sue, she had done it before, in Glasgow. In the Glasgow office the target of her 'Cupid's bow and arrow' was her best friend and fellow artist Nicky. Nicky was a fabulous-looking girl with a great personality, and yet Sue had failed to find her a suitable boyfriend. Instead, the two girls became best friends, and although Nicky still lived in Glasgow, they remained best friends. There would be hours of telephone conversations between Hutchinson & Bailey's Glasgow office and its London office without any business actually taking place. Sue kept Nicky up to date on her efforts with Trevor. She even suggested that Nicky should come down to London for a weekend and meet Trevor, whom she was sure Nicky would like. Nicky had heard that one before.

Sue unfortunately was having as little success with Trevor as she had had with Nicky in Glasgow. Weekend after weekend she would organise yet another foursome with herself and Tony, and time and time again none of the girls, although some of them were very beautiful, managed to tickle Trevor's fancy.

So it was that Trevor's first couple of months in the office in Bond Street were happy ones. However, outside the office things were not so great. Trevor had got himself accommodation, which was all it could be called, in Sussex Gardens. It was literally just a room with a shower and a television. There were no cooking facilities, no table big enough to open a sketch pad on, not even an armchair to relax in. Although his room was on the fifth floor, the only view he had from his window was of an adjacent building which seemed close enough to touch. Trevor called the place his 'cell'. He hated it, and began to feel very, very lonely for home. In an effort to alleviate this loneliness Trevor began to visit the Irish pubs, where he would take a few glasses with people from Ireland. They would sing rebel songs and tell exaggerated stories from home. But when the pub closed he would go back to his cell and to a landlord who didn't even speak English, and the loneliness would return. In his first couple of weeks he wrote home to his mother virtually every day. When the loneliness took a grip, this was the first thing that suffered. Fearful that his loneliness would come through in his writing, he began to write less frequently. He didn't want his mother to know that everything about life away wasn't perfect; no emigrant wants their mother to know that.

Chapter 8

IT WAS 3AM. DERMOT AND BUSTER were crouched behind the wall in the darkness. They rose slowly together, and peered over the wall. The house was in darkness, as Buster said it would be, and it looked deserted. Slowly they sank back down into their crouched positions. Burglary was not their forte, in fact it was hard to find a crime that *was* their forte.

'You're sure they're on holiday, Buster?' Dermot whispered.

'Yeh, Dermo, they're a circus family and they tour all summer. Then they take the winter months off. They're gone away for a month.'

'And there's no security? No alarm?' Dermot felt uncomfortable. This was all too easy, he thought.

Buster just shook his head and answered with a simple 'Nope.'

'Right then, let's go,' Dermot announced.

The two men vaulted the wall and the Boot Hill Gang went into action.

The Garibaldi home was a large, six-bedroomed house. It had taken the Garibaldis many years of working on the road with their circus to be able to afford such a home. They were indeed away for a month's holiday in Italy, leaving their home in the charge of two workmen who came every morning, checked over the house, mucked out the stables and fed the animals.

Dermot and Buster made their way slowly along a line of fir trees which led up to the outer buildings of the residence. When they came to the end of the trees they made a ten-yard dash on tiptoe to the corner of the larger building. It looked like a store-room of some kind.

'I wonder what's in here?' Dermot said softly to Buster, tilting his head towards the door of the building behind which they were hiding.

'I don't know. It must be valuable though,' Buster answered.

'Why?'

''Cause there's a lock on the door. Why would you lock a door if there was nothing valuable inside?' Buster declared with a thief's logic.

'You're right, Buster.'

The two men made their way slowly to the door. Gently, Dermot lifted the lock and examined it. He chuckled.

'It's an ordinary bleedin' barrel lock. I'll pick this quicker than pickin' me nose,' Dermot said as he took a tiny sliver of metal from his breast pocket and began to work. Within seconds the lock clicked open.

'You're a genius, Dermo,' Buster said, full of admiration.

'I know,' Dermot simply smiled.

The interior of the building was pitch dark, but warm. The two men felt around inside the doorway and could find no light switch. They began to search the building by touch.

'You go that way, I'll go this way,' Dermot whispered.

'Okay, Dermo,' Buster answered and then added, 'Dermot?'

'What?' Dermot asked impatiently.

'Which way am I supposed to go? I can't see which way you're pointin' in the dark.'

Buster felt himself being turned around by the shoulders and pushed. 'That fuckin' way.'

'Okay.'

Dermot had a box of matches in his pocket, but didn't want to strike a light unless he had too. As he felt his way around he felt some things that were familiar – a bale of straw, a rope of some sort, a shovel which he nearly fell over. Suddenly Buster called him from the far side of the room. 'Bingo, Dermot.'

'What? What is it?'

'I'm after findin' a fur coat!' Buster answered gleefully.

'Brilliant!' Dermot answered as he felt his way over to where Buster's voice had come from.

'Ah – maybe it's not brilliant,' Buster said in a very even voice.

'Why?'

'It's after lickin' me!' Buster answered with a rattle in his voice.

Dermot struck a match, and the two men were treated to a live performance of the MGM Studios trade mark. The growl of the lion couldn't even be heard above the screams of the two men.

Luckily for the Boot Hill Gang, Clarence, the Garibaldi family's oldest lion, had been fed that day. He didn't want to eat the men, he just wanted to play with them. Unfortunately for the Boot Hill Gang, lions have claws.

Shortly after being admitted to casualty at St Patrick's hospital, Buster Brady was rushed to the operating theatre where Dr Pat Watson spent the next three hours performing very delicate surgery upon him. By the end of it Dr Watson was very pleased with his work and was able to tell Dermot Browne that, given time and a bit of rest, Buster would make a full recovery. The only lasting sign of the evening's escapade would be that the Boot Hill Gang from that day onward would boast only three testicles between the two of them.

Dermot first 'phoned the Brady family and informed them that he and Buster had had an accident, but that everything was all right and that Buster would be fine. He then 'phoned Mark and asked him to come and collect him from the hospital and drive him back to Finglas. There was little conversation in the car during the trip home. Mark simply shook his head and said, 'One of these days, Dermot, I'm telling you, you two are going to go too far.'

Dermot didn't answer, he just stared out the window into space.

Back in the recovery room in St Patrick's hospital, Buster Brady too stared into space. Dr Watson had just broken the news to him, and Buster was trying to work out what a 'testicle' was.

Chapter 9

WITH ONLY DERMOT IN THE BOYS' BEDROOM Agnes saw little point in having five beds there, especially since it meant that Dermot was squeezed into a corner. She mentioned this to Pierre and he immediately volunteered to remove and store the extra beds, as well as centralise Dermot's bed. When Agnes accepted his offer, Pierre was quite surprised and delighted. He felt that this moved him a little closer to co-habitation, his ultimate goal. Early the following Monday morning, Pierre rolled up his sleeves and began to shift the furniture. Manoeuvring the beds down the narrow stairway on his own was difficult, and by the time he had the last bed out of the house, Pierre was pumping perspiration. He next pulled the mattress off Dermot's bed and moved it to the doorway at the top of the stairs. When he returned to the bed base he was greeted by a smiling brunette named Cheryl. She was standing with her hands propping up enormous naked breasts. Her brown eyes were staring at Pierre from the cover of *Mayfair* magazine, Dermot's bedside reading. Pierre lifted the magazine and began to flick through the pages. He then sat down on the edge of the bed base and began to read. He became most interested in an article which had the headline 'Turn me on, set me loose!' This was an in-depth look at what it was that turned normal women into 'sexual animals'. When he was only halfway through the article Pierre again began to perspire, and by the end of the article he had made up his mind. It was time to turn Agnes Browne into a 'sexual animal'.

*   *   *

Tony McMullen's knowledge of the hardware industry was the envy of many a counterhand at Lenehan's Hardware Store in Capel Street. In the years he had spent in the hardware business everything had passed through Tony McMullen's hands, from a torque wrench to carpentry pins the width of a human hair. He was indeed a valued senior member of counter staff in Lenehan's. Of course, Tony was like all men – just when you thought you had seen it all, something would come along and change all that. He scratched his head and once again began to flick through the stock book. He found the index page and scanned everything listed under the letter 'N'. No luck. It didn't help that the customer had a French accent and mumbled. He looked up again at the French man.

'Nipple clamps?' he asked, with a puzzled frown on his forehead.

'Eh yes, nipple clamps – eh, would you keep your voice down please?' Pierre answered.

McMullen closed the stock book and called across the counter. 'ARTHUR! Nipple clamps? Do we have any?'

Arthur, who had been showing an elderly lady where the starter fuse was inserted in a fluorescent light, stopped what he was doing and looked up at the ceiling as if expecting to find the answer to Tony's question there. He scratched under his chin, looked back at McMullen, shrugged and answered, 'I don't think so, Tony.'

A few of the younger customers stared at Pierre. Some began to giggle. McMullen wasn't giving up.

'Is it an oil nipple or a water nipple you want?'

'Breast. Breast nipples,' Pierre mumbled.

'Brist? What do you mean, brist?'

Pierre cupped his hand beneath his breast as he had seen Cheryl do in her cover pose. 'Breast nipples,' he said, pointing to an imaginary nipple about four inches out from his breast.

Tony McMullen's expression changed completely. Even his ears moved back as if pinned to the side of his head. His face reddened, with a mixture of embarrassment and anger. 'Now you listen, pal, perverts like you should be locked up! Now get your arse out of this shop.'

Pierre was confused. He was sure that this man was an adventurer like himself and just misunderstood how effective nipple clamps could be. 'No, no, it is not perverted. It is very pleasurable, let me show you.'

Pierre went to pinch McMullen's nipple. McMullen slapped his hand and now came around the counter.

'You try that again and I'll box the fuckin' head off you. Now, out!' he roared.

Pierre beat a retreat. He was more than a little shaken following the events in Lenehan's. However, he had less trouble purchasing the other items he needed from the Costume Shop and Saddlery. With all the pieces in place, except for the nipple clamps of course, Pierre looked forward to transforming Agnes into a sexual animal. He even had an idea for replacing the nipple clamps which he believed was quite creative, and was very proud of his

67

lateral thinking. Pierre arrived that evening at Agnes's house with three bottles of champagne cider, a bouquet of flowers, and smelling like the Avon Lady's briefcase. Agnes was thrilled by this gesture. It was just what she needed. Her mind had been preoccupied of late by the disintegration of her family and she was feeling very low and, to be honest, unwanted.

The evening began wonderfully. They put on some soft music and the first two bottles of cider vanished quickly. Agnes poured her heart out to Pierre. About how she felt her family was falling apart, and how she blamed herself. Pierre tried to explain that this is the way families are meant to go. Children become adults, and adults must go their own way and make a life for themselves. His explanations fell on stony ground, for Agnes argued that it was possible for them to become adults and still retain the family unit, even though they were scattered or married or whatever. As the evening wore on, the fire in the hearth began to die, and Agnes's thoughts turned to bed, exactly where Pierre's thoughts had been from the moment he had walked in the door. Agnes drained her glass and, collecting up her purse, cigarettes and lighter, stood up.

'Are you going to stay the night, Pierre?' she asked.

'I would love to,' Pierre answered, with a playful leer in his voice.

'Oh, I see,' Agnes answered equally playfully. 'Well, come on then, lover boy,' and she giggled.

'You go up first, I will follow.' Pierre was getting excited, for his moment was coming.

'What?' Agnes was puzzled.

'Go on. I have a little surprise for you.'

Agnes went on up to the bedroom. She was tickled with anticipation. She stripped and changed her underwear, donning her good Playtex bra. She got into bed and settled herself. When she could hear Pierre's footsteps ascending the stairs she turned towards the wall, leaving her back facing the door. She did this because she knew Pierre would begin by kissing her all over her back, and she liked that.

She couldn't see the tears in Pierre's eyes as he entered the room. Tears or no tears, Pierre was determined to see this through!

It was the crack of the bull-whip that removed the smile of anticipation from Agnes's face. She turned slowly to see what had made the noise.

'Sweet loving Jesus!' were the words that came from her lips as she half-sat, frozen at the sight that lay before her.

'Come, you sexual animal,' Pierre said in a guttural voice.

'Have you gone fuckin' mad, Pierre?' Agnes now stood out of bed face-to-face with Pierre, who was naked except for a Lone Ranger mask and two plastic clothes pegs, one of which he wore on each nipple. Pierre let out a theatrical laugh and cracked the bull-whip again. The bull-whip ripped a large gash in the net curtains on its outward journey and burst the pillow on its return journey, sending feathers billowing around the bedside light.

'Come on, sexy! I hit you then you hit me, Agnes baby.' Except for the name, this was a direct quote from 'Turn me on, set me loose'.

'Right! Me first!' Agnes roared.

Agnes's right cross to Pierre's chin bent him nearly completely backwards. He tried hard to stay on his feet, swinging his arms in an effort to counter-balance his arched form. There was a sharp 'click-click' as the two plastic pegs released their grip on Pierre's now blue nipples and with a slight smile of relief he buckled into unconsciousness.

In fairness, Agnes embellished the story a little more when she retold it the next day to the other stall holders in Moore Street's market. Carmel Dowdall laughed so much that she had to slip away to Guiney's to buy a new pair of knickers, after wetting the ones she came to work in when Agnes reached the point in the story where she described the two clothes pegs and Pierre's blue nipples. For his part, Pierre du Gloss learned that turning Agnes Browne on was one thing, but setting her loose was dangerous!

Chapter 10

TREVOR WAS SITTING ALONE IN THE ART ROOM. It was lunch time. He had decided not to take a lunch break but instead to finish the illustration he was working on. It felt weird to be working on Christmas scenes while the autumn sun was beaming through the window. But in the advertising world today was old news, everybody worked on tomorrow. The ring of the 'phone on Sue White's desk was like a fire alarm, and jarred Trevor's thoughts awake. He let it ring for a few moments in the hope that whoever it was would realise it was lunch time and hang up. They didn't. So he answered the 'phone. It was Nicky in Glasgow.

'Hello?' Trevor said softly.

'Hello. Who's that?' Her voice was nice.

'Hutchinson & Bailey,' Trevor answered.

'I know that, who are you?'

'Sorry. It's Trevor, Trevor Browne, I'm an artist here.'

'Ah, so you're Trevor.' The young woman laughed.

'I beg your pardon?'

'Oh, I'm sorry, Trevor. This is Nicky in Glasgow. I was looking for Sue.'

'Oh! She's not here, she's gone out, I'm afraid ... em, Nicky.' For no reason Trevor blushed.

'She's probably gone looking for another date for you!' Nicky announced. This time they both laughed.

'She keeps you up to date then, Nicky?' Trevor relaxed.

'I know *exactly* what you're going through, Trevor. I was her victim for two years while she was here in Scotland. She means well though. She really does.'

'Oh I know that, in fact, and don't tell her this, some of the girls were really nice, it's not them it's just – well – yeh know.'

'You wouldn't believe how I know. Listen, Trevor, tell her I called and that I'll call her later, okay?'

'Okay,' he answered with a smile. Slowly Trevor returned the handset to its cradle. He liked her.

Sue was the last to return to the art room from lunch. Whatever had happened on her lunch break, it had her in a very happy mood. Then she and Tony had a few quiet words, and that seemed to change her mood completely. Trevor wondered what it was that had made her so happy and now so sad. At the four o'clock tea break he would find out.

'I spent my lunch hour,' Sue began, 'driving out to look at a place in Cookham. It's gorgeous, Trevor. A three-bedroomed house, right behind a country pub called The Swan Uppers. The back garden sweeps down to the Thames, and it's right beside a golf course – you know how much Tony likes golf?' Sue really was enthusiastic.

'Yes, I do. It sounds great, so what's the problem?'

Trevor's question stopped Sue in her tracks. She hung her head for a moment, and when she brought it up again she looked across the room at Tony with the expression of a child who had just had her favourite toy stolen. In a disappointed tone she announced, 'Tony says it's too expensive to rent.'

'And is it?' Trevor asked.

Sue looked at him like he had just joined the enemy ranks. 'Yes!' The conversation was over.

Trevor had arranged to have a drink with Tony and Sue after work that evening. They often did this. Straight after shutting down for the day they would head around the corner to a tiny little pub called Mrs Muffin's. There they would have a few drinks, a few laughs and talk shop for a couple of hours. Trevor wasn't looking forward to this evening. Tony and Sue were fabulous company, unless they were fighting. When quitting time came, Sue was not in the art room. She had gone up to Mr Bailey's office to make a presentation on a new soft drinks concept she had. She had already been up there for two hours, which generally meant the presentation was going well. Tony left a little note on her desk saying that he and

Trevor would be waiting in Mrs Muffin's and the two men headed off to the pub.

'Two pints of mild,' Tony called, before returning to the main topic of conversation with Trevor. 'A hundred and twenty-five pounds a week is just out of the question, Trevor. Oh, we could manage it all right, but then I wouldn't be able to save. If I can't save then there would be no money for our own place, for when we get married.'

'You two are getting married?' Trevor asked the question not because he was surprised that Sue and Tony might marry, but the way Tony had said it, it sounded like they were getting married the next day.

'Well, yes – eventually, I hope. I haven't asked Sue yet, but I'm sure we will, what do you think?' he asked.

Trevor got a little flustered at being asked such a momentous question by someone who to all intents and purposes was a stranger. So he drew on one of his mother's sayings.

'I'll tell you, Tony, when God made you two he matched you,' then he raised his glass to Tony. Maybe it was the clink of the glasses, or maybe Trevor really did hear a little bell going off in his head. Whatever it was, what was about to happen next was totally out of character for Trevor. He was not a spontaneous man, yet on this occasion as the thought struck him he spoke it out loud. 'Maybe I could help?'

Tony was in mid-mouthful, and he swallowed and wiped his lips. 'What do you mean?'

Trevor had started so now he had to finish. 'What if I were to share in this house in Cookham? I could chip in forty pounds a week, no problem. You would actually be doing me a favour because I hate the kip I'm living in now. I wouldn't be in the way or anything, would I?'

Tony slowly ran his finger around the rim of his pint glass and stared into the froth. After a few moments he looked up at Trevor. 'You wouldn't be in *our* way, but are you sure you want to do this? I mean this place has a one-year lease, that would mean you're stuck with us for a year at least.'

'If I have to be stuck with someone for a year, I can't think of anybody else I'd rather be stuck with than you and Sue.'

As if by magic at the mention of her name, Sue entered Mrs Muffin's. The presentation had obviously gone well, and she seemed to have got over her mid-afternoon disappointment over Cookham. Once she had a drink in her hand, Tony wasted no time.

'Sue, if we are to move to this place in Cookham, we really can't afford it on our own, but we could take in a lodger!'

'Thanks, Tony, I know you mean well, but I've been thinking about it. You're right, we can't afford it, and as much as I love the place I don't fancy living with a stranger.'

Trevor went to speak but was stopped by a sharp wink from Tony.

'What if...' Tony began, 'the stranger was our Trevor here?' Tony was only short of pushing his tongue into his cheek as he spoke, for he already knew the reaction this would bring from Sue.

Sue didn't speak. Instead she snapped a look at Trevor. Trevor simply smiled and nodded his head. There followed a burst of laughter from the three and a group hug.

Chapter 11

VERY FEW OF US REALLY UNDERSTAND or witness the full consequences of our 'pranks'. This was particularly true of Dermot and Buster. For instance, sitting in a café, Dermot would pour the contents of the salt cellar into the sugar and leave. He would not know that the elderly woman who would use their table next would be violently sick following her first mouthful of salted coffee. Or that this sickness would have an adverse effect on the reputation of the café and its owner, who struggled every day to make the business pay. To Dermot and Buster it was just a giggle. But sometimes, consequences do catch up with us, and they did for Dermot Browne and Buster Brady on the night of 17 September 1981.

Dermot had never seen Mary Carter look so ill. When they were sitting in the bar of Foley's pub her co-ordination was so bad that she couldn't even pick up her glass. She was loud and boisterous, and Dermot was getting embarrassed at being the focal point of all the other customers in the bar. Mr Foley's insistence to Dermot that he get her out of there only just pre-empted Dermot's own thoughts on the matter. He half-walked, half-carried her back to her flat, where he left her asleep on the couch before returning to Foley's. He now sat beside Buster and was very quiet.

'She just overdone it a bit, Dermo,' Buster offered by way of consolation.

'Yeh, sure, Buster.'

'She'll be all right in the morning.'

'Yeh, sure she will, Buster.'

The two young men were sitting on the high stools at the bar. This was more comfortable for Buster, who, since his testicular surgery, had difficulty in sitting on a low seat and bending his midriff. There was something nagging at Dermot. While he was taking Mary Carter back to her flat, she was ranting and raving and coming out with all kinds of gobbledegook, most of which Dermot didn't understand. But when they reached her flat and he was laying her on the couch, there could be no mistaking what she said. She spoke in a flat tone but it was quite clear. 'Easy, Dermo, don't hurt the baby.'

The words swam in his head. He didn't mention anything to Buster. Instead, with a wave of his hand, he ordered two more pints from Mr Foley, who was only delighted to be serving Dermot and Buster on their own. The next round would be accompanied by two small Irish whiskeys. The two young men proceeded to drink themselves into oblivion.

By half-past midnight the two of them were standing outside Shakers nightclub. Dermot stood away from the door, leaning against the lamp post, using the lamp post as most Irish men use history – for support rather than illumination. Meanwhile, Buster was talking to the doormen and trying to convince them that he and Dermot were two overseas salesmen just out for the evening. The doormen were very experienced, although they didn't need to be too experienced to know that not too many overseas salesmen had Manchester United tattooed on their right arm and spoke with strong Dublin accents. The doorman tried the tactful way at first, telling Buster that only a certain kind of person in a certain kind of dress was allowed into the club. Buster's reply to this was, 'Is that why they make you two gorillas stand outside?'

The doormen then resorted to the standard doorman's farewell. 'You're not getting in, pal, so fuck off.'

They stumbled along up the east side of Parnell Square, Buster telling Dermot how lucky the bouncers were that Buster happened to be in a good humour, otherwise he would have killed them. By the time they had reached Frederick Street they had attempted to wave down at least twenty taxi cabs. Some of the cabs were already occupied and those that weren't had drivers experienced enough to know drunks when they saw them. When they reached Mountjoy Square they scrambled through a gap in the railings surrounding the park in an effort to get into the bushes and relieve themselves. Buster finished first and as Dermot was completing his shakes he could hear Buster in the distance calling to him.

'Hey, Dermo, push me, come on, push me!'

Dermot followed the voice and came out of the bushes to see Buster sitting on one of the swings in the children's playground. He began to laugh aloud and ran to Buster and began pushing him. Buster went higher and higher with each push until at the apex of one of the swings Buster threw up and on the downward swing it looked like he was breathing fire.

'Ah, stop me, Dermo, stop me, please,' was now the cry.

Dermot tried to put his hands in front of him to stop the swing but the power of Buster's return went straight past his hands and the swing seat caught him above the eye, knocking him straight off his feet onto his back. Buster, in an effort to turn in the swing to see what had happened to Dermot, shot straight off the seat and landed twenty feet away from where Dermot lay. The two men groaned for a while and then, raising themselves onto their elbows, looked across at each other. The burst of laughter was spontaneous. Buster's face was grazed all down the left side and Dermot had a bump on the top of his forehead the length and width of a good Havana cigar. They got to their feet and made their way out of the park laughing. They leaned against the park railings until the laughter subsided. Then Dermot had the idea. He raised his left arm and pointed. 'Buster, d'you see what I see?'

Buster's gaze followed Dermot's finger. 'What?' Buster asked.

'The bus depot!'

'So?'

'Where there's a bus depot there's buses.' Dermot's voice was now slurred, and the word buses sounded like 'bushes', but still Buster understood what he meant. Still, he repeated his question. 'So?'

'So, let's go and get ourselves a bus!' And Dermot headed off into the night.

Buster stood for a moment with a frown on his face and then it dawned on him. He gathered himself and tottered after Dermot.

'That's a great idea, Dermo. I want to be the conductor.'

Although it was the early hours of the morning a few of the walkers tried to stop the bus as it wove its way along the Glasnevin Road. Dermot had had a bit of difficulty in hot-wiring the bus, but once he had it up and running he found it as easy to drive as a truck, and even more fun. Buster was upstairs with a handful of coins walking up and down the seats clicking the coins and talking to imaginary passengers. Every now and then he would ring the bus bell and roar down the stairs, 'Plenty of room on top,' sending Dermot into fits of laughter.

Dermot had driven big trucks before, but he had never driven anything with power-steering. He tended to over-compensate on the turns and this caused the bus to weave. At the bottom of Glasnevin Hill they were really moving. The road took a sharp right as it went over the Tolka river bridge and up the hill onto the Finglas Road. As he rounded the bend, Dermot over-compensated and the bus swung to the left. He pulled the wheel sharply to the left in an effort to straighten the swing. He pulled the wheel too much. The bus went into a spin and skidded sideways. Buster toppled head-over-heels and got wedged between two seats, which probably saved his life. Smoke billowed from the wheels which were now locked, with Dermot's foot firmly on the brake. The rear wheels mounted the kerb first, which made the front spin around faster. The front wheels hopped up on the kerb. It seemed like the bus was never going to stop, but it did. It all felt like slow motion to Dermot – he saw the block wall come towards him and the bus crashed into it at an angle right at the driver's seat. Five of the upstairs windows had shattered when the bus mounted the kerb, all but two of the remaining windows in the bus went into smithereens as soon as it crashed into the wall. Then there was silence.

First of all there was darkness, then in the distance Dermot heard the ding-ding of a bell. Then he could hear Buster's voice, but couldn't make out what the voice was saying. He had a sharp pain in his right leg. He shook his head as if to clear it and it worked – he could hear Buster's voice much more clearly now. Buster was still upstairs in the bus, talking to his imaginary passengers.

'This is as far as we go, folks. Everybody off here,' Buster was crying out loud as he made his way unsteadily down the stairs. 'Dermo, Dermo, are you all right, Dermo?'

Dermot was wondering the same thing himself. He felt around his body, and nothing seemed to be broken. There was blood on his face from the tiny cuts that the shattering glass had made. But other than that there seemed to be nothing serious. His right leg was wedged in the buckled metal just above the peddles. It wouldn't move. Within seconds Buster was by his side.

'I'm stuck, Buster,' Dermot said.

'Where?' Buster asked.

Dermot pointed downwards to the bottom of his right leg. Buster half-lay down, manoeuvring his foot in behind Dermot's leg to where the buckled metal was. With a grunt, he pushed as hard as he could on the metal, held it for as long as he could, and then relaxed.

'Any good?'

'Yeh, I think it will work, try again.' Dermot was in more than a little pain.

Buster tried again, this time putting all of the weight that he could onto the metal. With a jerk, Dermot's foot came free, but without the shoe. They climbed off the bus. There was still total silence all around them.

'Let's get the fuck out of here, Buster, the law will be here any minute. Over there across the field,' Dermot was pointing to a gap in a ditch.

The two men made their way to the gap, negotiated the ditch and found themselves in a field that ran behind a dairy. Slowly they made their way home. It could have been nerves, but after about twenty minutes walking the two of them started to giggle.

'There's no doubt about it, Buster, when we do it we do it in style.' The two men laughed.

'Janey, Dermot, when the manager of that bus depot comes in in the morning he won't be too happy.'

The fact was, in the morning there would be very few people happy, for Mark Browne's prediction about his brother's pranks was about to come true.

*   *   *

John Cullen had been a barman for fifty-one years. He had started when he was just fourteen years old in Miley's pub in Galvaston, his home village just outside Mullingar. In the half-century his career had spanned, he had worked in bars in virtually every county in Ireland, before his current position as assistant bar manager in The Widow's public house in Main Street, Finglas. For his sixty-five years, he was a fit man. He attributed his fitness to the fact that he drank little, smoked only pipe tobacco, and cycled to and from work every day. John Cullen had a full driving licence although he never thought he would use it now. He was wrong. The owners of The Widow's public house, and its long-standing customers, had had a fund-raising drive and had raised enough money for a 'new' second-hand car to present to John on his retirement in two weeks' time. Cycling, John would tell anyone who would listen, had its advantages. There were no traffic problems to contend with. It was good for your health, and, he would add with a laugh, if you were caught short all you had to do was park your bike somewhere and find a bush or a wall to relieve yourself behind. This is exactly what he had done on that night coming home from The Widow's. He was standing behind the block wall, one arm up against it, with his head down to ensure that he wasn't soiling his shoes when he heard the tyre screeches across the road. This was followed by two bangs and the sound of breaking glass.

'What the hell is that?' were the last words that came from the lips of John Cullen as the bus crashed through the wall, which disintegrated on top of him. His death, his widow was later told, was immediate.

Chapter 12

'WOULD THE ACCUSED PLEASE STAND.' Justice McCarthy spoke loudly and deliberately.

Dermot Browne and Buster Brady slowly took to their feet and stared at the jury in an effort to garner some hint of their fate. It had been reasonably short for a manslaughter trial. Most of the nine days were taken up with evidence from the bouncers in Shakers nightclub, from Mr Foley, from a courting couple who had seen Dermot and Buster playing in the playground of Mountjoy Square and from the night watchman at the dairy, who saw Dermot and Buster hobble across the field. There were only two witnesses for the defense: Dermot Browne and Buster Brady, although the police did make much of the fact that Dermot Browne had handed himself in to the police station on the morning following Mr Cullen's death.

Giving himself up was his mother's idea. The morning after the crash, when Dermot heard that John Cullen had died in the accident, his immediate reaction was to run. He and Buster hadn't returned to their homes that night, but had gone instead to Chestnut Hole, where they had both bedded down. It was the next morning, while they were having a cup of coffee in a café in Finglas village and the death of John Cullen was being discussed at a table next to them, that they realised that *they* had been the perpetrators.

Buster panicked. 'Jaysus, Dermo, they're going to get us this time.'

'Shut up, Buster, they don't know who it was, now shut up.'

'Ah they'll find out, Dermo, they'll find out.'

Dermot grabbed Buster by the collar. 'Will you stay fuckin' quiet.' Dermot thought quickly. 'First things first, Buster. You get to a public 'phone and ring your house, make sure nobody has been up there. If the police haven't been there yet, then it's because nobody saw us. Anybody will tell you, unless things like this are solved in the first twenty-four hours they rarely ever get solved, so keep the head!'

'But what if they have been up there, Dermo?'

'Then, Buster, you and me are gonna have to get out of town, get out of the country!'

Buster was sniffling as he left the table to make his way to a public 'phone box. Dermot ordered another coffee and waited. Fifteen minutes later Buster returned. Dermot didn't have to ask him any questions, for as he entered through the café swing doors his face was deathly white. He quickly slid into the cubicle facing Dermot.

'The police were up this morning at your house and my house, Dermo. It was the security man from the dairy, Paddy Reilly – he recognised us. What'll we do?' Buster began to cry softly.

Dermot's instinct was to grab Buster and tell him to calm down, but instead he gently put his hand on Buster's arm. 'Hey, Buster, it's all right. If the worst comes to the worst it was my idea and nothing to do with you. But I still think we should have a go at getting out of here.'

Buster looked at Dermot. He felt as if he were going to be physically sick. Dermot paid for the coffees and they left the café, making their way back to Chestnut Hole, the long way through Mackey's field so as not to have to go past the police station. When they got to Chestnut Hole, Dermot went to his 'hidey hole' to see how much money he had to go on the run with. He raised his hand to remove the brick but noticed that it was already halfway out. Someone had been at his 'hidey hole'. He took the brick down and there in front of him at eye-level was an envelope marked 'Dermot'.

'What's that?' Buster asked.

'I don't know,' Dermot said softly as he tore the envelope open. The first thing that caught his eye was the bunch of used pound notes. There was a hundred and seventy-five pounds in all. The money was accompanied by a letter. Dermot opened the letter and began to read. It was from his mother.

Dear Dermot,

This is a dread full thing that has happened. The police were here at six o'clock this morning and they spoke about you like you were scum. I told them you were at times a little divil but that you would never hurt anyone on purpose. They wouldnt listen they didnt want to know and they talked about you as if you were a murderer. Dermot I know this was an accident and I know as well that you are proberly thinking of running away now. Im asking you as your mother and somebody who loves you dearly to do the right thing and give yourself up so as everyone will know that this was an accident but its up to you. Your a big lad now. If you decide not to give yourself up and go on the run I have enclosed all the money I could lay my hands on. I hope it will help you. Wherever you go please get in touch with me and let me know that your okay.

Mammy
PS: They are looking for Buster too.

Dermot slowly lowered the letter. His eyes were filled but not one tear fell.

Buster looked into his face questioningly. 'What'll we do, Dermo?'

Dermot put his arm around Buster's shoulder and softly said, 'Come on, Buster, let's go home.'

He returned the money to his mother, gave her a hug and a kiss, and by midday he and Buster had surrendered themselves at Finglas Garda Station.

'We, the jury, find the defendants, Dermot Browne and Patrick Brady, guilty of manslaughter in the second degree.' Dermot and Buster had both been expecting a guilty verdict. But it was like having somebody you love on their death-bed for a long time with a terminal illness – when the death finally comes it isn't any easier. The word 'guilty' echoed through Dermot's mind. He took a look across at the gallery to see his family's reaction. Agnes was distraught, and her head was buried in Mark's shoulder. Mark stared at him. He was angry. His sister Cathy stood with a blank look on her face; her husband Mick half-sneered at Dermot. Dermot's twin brother Simon was pale and sad-looking, and Rory was shaking, as he was being consoled by Dino Doyle. Two seats away from his family was a sight Dermot hadn't expected to see. Mary Carter stared at him, her eyes wide and tears streaming down her face, and when she saw that he was looking at her she gave him a little wave. Dermot just shrugged.

Chapter 13

TREVOR SLOWLY PUT HIS MOTHER'S LETTER DOWN on the bedside table. He felt awful. The letter was full of bad news. 'Seven years.' He spoke Dermot's sentence out loud. He was glad for once that he wasn't at home. He couldn't imagine the anguish his mother must be going through, as well as Dermot. He knew how his mother would take the worry on board as if she herself were to serve the sentence. Cathy was due her baby any day now and Agnes had hinted in the letter that all was not well there either. His mother had talked about coming over to visit him, to give herself a break. He must remember to ask Sue and Tony if it was okay that she stay here with them in the new house.

He was happier now than he had ever been since he had come to England. Cookham was beautiful. The move so far out of the city had meant that they all had to rise a lot earlier to get the early train into London, but it was worth it, for at the weekends Trevor could spend his time walking for miles and miles, through the golf course or along the banks of the Thames. He would park his easel in a different spot each Sunday and paint until the sun went down. Sue and Tony loved the place, although Sue wasn't quite becoming the mother hen that Tony thought she would. She filled the house with her childlike giggles and Tony would get tense and ask her to behave more like an adult. Sue would simply shrug and tell Tony to 'get a life'. Still, most of the time the two were just simply in love, and although Trevor sometimes felt like the odd man out he never felt like a gooseberry.

'Seven years – Jesus Christ!' Trevor lay back on the pillow, his hands behind his head, and stared at the ceiling.

* * *

Four hundred miles away in Mountjoy Prison, Dermot Browne was also lying on his back, staring at the ceiling. He could just about make it out, for the cell was in darkness. It was way past 'lights out' and Dermot still wasn't asleep. There are no words that can describe the downward tumble you feel when your world goes from encompassing everything you see to twelve foot by six foot of mass concrete. The tiny window from Dermot's cell in C-block overlooked the exercise yard. This would be his view for the next seven years.

Not since the day he was first locked up had Dermot initiated a conversation with anyone – not even with Buster, who was in the same block but a floor below. His nights were spent mostly lying awake; if he was lucky he would get one or two hours' sleep. Instead, he spent his nights just thinking. He thought about his mother – he would imagine her every night taking out the mugs, pouring the tea, and settling herself down at the kitchen table for the nightly chat with them all. She had no-one now. He thought about his sister Cathy, how unwell she had looked in the courtroom and the pale colour of her face. He tried not to worry that her husband was treating her badly; he couldn't afford to worry. In prison you just can't allow yourself to worry because you can do nothing about what's happening on the outside. He thought about Buster – three years as an accessory. He'd be out in a little over one year. Dermot was glad that Buster had got it a little easy. He thought about his brother Mark and how everything always seemed to go the right way for him – or was it that Mark just always did the right thing? He thought about Rory – homosexual or not, at least he had someone who loved him in Dino, and tonight they would probably go to the pictures or whatever and if they were lying like himself on a bed in the darkness staring at the ceiling it would be from choice. But mostly he thought about Mary Carter. The baby couldn't be his. He was sure he wasn't the only one Mary Carter had slept with in the past few months, and yet the thought of her being with another man filled him with rage. He couldn't understand this, he didn't know what caused it. But he told himself that the baby just couldn't be his.

These were the things that filled all of his thoughts each night, except for one more thing. At the end of each night he would think of a woman alone – the widow Cullen. She would be alone tonight and every other night for the rest of her life because Dermot had gone too far. Dermot closed his eyes and sobbed quietly.

*   *   *

As is often the case with long-term prisoners, Dermot refused visitors for his first few weeks. The majority of long-term prisoners would usually have had a couple of short visits to prison before a big sentence, for smaller crimes before the 'big one'. This enabled them to get used to prison life before they had to serve a long sentence. But this was not the case for Dermot. He had a dreadful time settling in and became completely withdrawn. It was sad for Buster, for if ever he needed his best friend, it was now. When he found himself ignored by Dermot he felt alone and afraid.

However, Buster took to prison life a lot quicker than Dermot did. He even started taking some of the courses that were available in the prison education scheme. He began to do leather work, then woodwork, but the course he enjoyed most was a letter-writing course. Here Buster learned how to construct sentences and how to place those sentences in such a way as to give structure to a letter. He found it challenging but enjoyable. Unfortunately for Buster, his letter-writing course became somewhat akin to playing table tennis alone, for the only address Buster had to write to was his home address, and neither his mother nor father would reply to any of his letters. So he wrote instead to Dermot's mother. Agnes replied, but only once in the blue moon. Father Gibney, the prison chaplain, lined up a couple of pen-friends for Buster, but soon they too stopped writing.

Dermot, on the other hand, received at least two letters a week from his mother. She tried her best to keep them lighthearted and full of local news and gossip, and would read them over and over to herself before posting them to ensure that her writing didn't reflect how desperately she was missing him. Initially Dermot didn't reply, as he felt he had nothing to say, but as time wore on he began to write at least one letter a fortnight home. When eventually he wrote that he would like to see Agnes on a visit, she was delighted. She arrived in the visiting room with a carton of cigarettes, some fresh fruit, and a few bags of liquorice allsorts, Dermot's favourite sweets. The visit went reasonably well, although Agnes was taken aback at how pale Dermot had become in just three months of incarceration. She tried not to show her shock and joked about how much weight he was losing. During the thirty minutes they spent together, Agnes spoke virtually without taking a breath, for she was afraid that if she stopped talking either one or both of them would begin to cry. Once they had got through the first visit, subsequent visits became easier and Agnes noticed that Dermot started to seem a little brighter each time. He was still very intense and withdrawn though, and Agnes continued to worry for his well-being.

In his first year of imprisonment, Agnes visited Dermot on eight occasions. Thanks to her visits, Dermot was able to share in the major events in the Browne family. It was Agnes that brought him the news of the birth of Simon's son, Thomas. She spent the entire half-hour visit speaking of how beautiful the baby was and her excitement in the telling of the story sent Dermot back to his cell that day feeling better than he had felt at any time since he had come to prison. On another visit, Agnes described every inch of the interior of the new direct-sales store Mark had opened for Senga Furnishings on the south side of Dublin. Like his mother, Dermot was thrilled for Mark, although on that day the sparkle in her eye as she recounted Mark's progress made Dermot feel dirty.

Just as a blind man has a heightened sense of hearing, when you are imprisoned and not affected on a daily basis by the hustle and bustle of the outside world you become extremely sensitive to people's body language. At the end of each of Agnes's visits, Dermot would always feel a little unsettled. He felt sure that Agnes was holding something back. He couldn't imagine what it was, and often in his letters and indeed in Agnes's visits he would probe into areas that he thought might be the cause of it, but to no avail. He sensed Agnes's tension even in the early visits, caused by her worrying about Cathy and how things were going for her down in Arklow. Like Agnes, Dermot suspected that Mick O'Leary might be giving his sister a hard time and that Cathy was covering it up. When he questioned Agnes about this, she readily admitted her fears. They had spent a long time discussing it quite openly, so openly in fact that Dermot realised that although Agnes had not discussed it previously so as not to worry Dermot, this was not the 'thing' that she was holding back. It was on her ninth visit to Mountjoy that Agnes was to reveal the *thing*, and Dermot stumbled upon it quite by accident. They were about midway through the visit when Dermot asked, 'Tell me, Ma, have you heard how Mary Carter is doin'?'

'Mary Carter?' Agnes answered as if she was hearing the name for the first time. The tone of voice and the sudden quick movement of her eyes told Dermot immediately this was the *thing*, and Dermot suddenly burst out with, 'Ah ha! So *that's* it!'

Agnes became flustered and even blushed. 'That's what? What are you talking about?'

'You've been visitin' her, haven't you?'

'The odd time.'

Neither spoke for a few minutes and Dermot rolled and lit up another cigarette. He became agitated now, turning sideways in the chair and crossing his legs, looking at Agnes half-over his shoulder.

'Did she have the baby?' Dermot finally asked.

'Yes. It's a boy. She's called him Cormac,' Agnes answered flatly.

Dermot exhaled a long stream of smoke. 'Cormac, yeh? That's a nice name.'

Agnes didn't speak.

'He's not mine, Mammy!' Dermot said this without looking at Agnes. She didn't reply.

Dermot turned and placed his elbows on the visitor's table and, looking straight at Agnes, he repeated his statement, this time more slowly. 'He's not mine, Mammy!'

'Okay,' Agnes replied without even raising her head.

'What do you mean, okay?'

'I mean okay. If you say he's not yours, okay! What do you want me to say?'

'I want you to say something like, of course he isn't, or yes, son, I know he's not yours, or – anything, but Jesus Christ, Mammy, *okay?*' Dermot's frustration was now starting to show and his voice was getting louder. In the background a warder lifted his head, moved off his stool and began to walk slowly towards their table.

'How can I say all that? I've held Cormac in me arms, Dermot. I've looked down into his face. He looks up at me, smiling, and what do I see? I see you. As you were in my arms twenty-five years ago. If he's not yours, Dermot Browne, then you've a double going around Dublin somewhere that's after fathering that child.'

'It could be anyone's! She's a junkie, for fuck sake, mother.' Dermot stood up as he said this and his chair flew back. His voice was near screaming pitch.

Agnes also stood up and pushed her face across the table towards his. 'Yes, she is, God love her. But she's trying her best to be a mother and with no help from anyone! The least she could expect is a little decency and recognition from the father of her child.'

The warder was now standing behind Dermot, but didn't know what to do.

Dermot lowered his tone. 'Oh you'd love that, wouldn't you? You'd love me to be just like Mark, wouldn't you?'

'No, son. I don't want you to be just like Mark, but I don't want you to be just like your father either!' Agnes cried.

Dermot drew his arm back as if to swing a punch. Now the warder knew exactly what to do. He flung himself at Dermot and in one practised movement, threw Dermot to the ground, lying on top of him. The warder was quickly joined by two colleagues who restrained Dermot on the ground.

Agnes screamed at them. 'Christ, don't hurt him, please don't hurt him.'

Another visitor came to Agnes's side and began to escort her to the exit. As they got to the door Agnes was crying. She looked back and saw Dermot, who was standing now but handcuffed, being bundled away. He was red with rage and there were tears streaming down his face.

'Don't come again, Mammy. I don't want to see you again. I mean it, don't come again,' Dermot roared as they dragged him through the steel door back into the cell blocks.

Chapter 14

OVER THE NEXT FEW WEEKS Agnes wrote a total of ten letters to Dermot. In each one she apologised for her behaviour, and for upsetting him, but emphasised that she did not apologise for what she had said. She received no reply, until one morning the postman delivered a large brown envelope with a Mountjoy Prison stamp on it. When she opened the envelope she found all her letters inside, torn in half, but unopened. She never wrote to Dermot again. Instead she began writing to Buster Brady, explaining to Buster what had happened and asking him to keep her informed of Dermot's progress. She asked Buster not to tell Dermot that she had been asking, lest he and Buster fall out. Buster's letters kept Agnes abreast of how Dermot was doing and although she missed the direct contact she was always glad of any news Buster had to impart.

From Buster's point of view it was a great arrangement. His letter-writing was coming on and he looked forward to sitting down and writing a letter to which he knew he would get a reply. Although Buster's letter-writing skills had improved, his grasp of the English language was still very loose, as, indeed, was Agnes's. This led to some rather peculiar exchanges, copies of some of which, to this day, can probably be found in the miscellaneous drawer in the Mountjoy Prison Censor's office. For instance, the following exchange of letters took place over a period of two weeks:

C Block
Mountjoy Prison
North Circular Road
Dublin 7

February 23rd 1983

Dear Mrs. Browne,

I am in receipt of yours of the 18th inst. Thank you for the reciep for Gur Cake, which I have passed on to 'Hatchet' Flannigan in the kitchen. Dermot is doing well. As I have said before he has his up days and his down days. Today is one of his up days, I can tell because this morning when I said good morning Dermot he did not tell me to fuck off. I have been here a long time and I still do not like it here and would like to be home. It is difficult to make friends here. Its like you are just getting to know someone and they are gone. This pyrole is a pain in the arse.

I hope this letter finds you as it left me, in good health.

Yours sincerely
Buster Brady.

Agnes read this letter over and over again, but still couldn't figure out what 'pyrole' was. When she showed it to Pierre, Pierre suggested that as the word was in the same sentence as 'pain in the arse' he could be talking about piles. Agnes was delighted that Pierre had figured out the puzzle and that she could do something about it!

43, Wolfe Tone Grove
Finglas
Dublin 11

February 27th 1983

Dear Buster,

Thank you very much for yet another letter, they are so important and I look forward to them. Your mother and father are well. They were delighted when I told them that you are due out at the end of next month, but said to tell you not to come home. I am sorry about that Buster, Ive tried hard but your mother talks about prison as if it were a disease.

Everybody is well here. Young Aaron is getting bigger by the day and although he is only two and a half he could pass for four. Rory and Dino are still talking about opening their own salon, but the only thing they have done so far is each others hair. Simon and Fiona are getting a house together in Raheny, I am delighted as this will give young Thomas a garden to play in, I never liked that bloody flat. I have not heard from Cathy in a while, so I cant give you any news about her. Why dont you write to her yourself? I have enclosed her address on a piece of card.

Well thats all for now Buster, I look forward to your next letter.

All my love,
Agnes Browne.

P.S. I am sorry to hear about your pyrole, nothing is worse than a pain in the arse. I have sent a package with this letter containing some suppositories, these should make you feel better.

C Block
Mountjoy Prison
North Circular Road
Dublin 7

March 3rd 1983

Dear Mrs. Browne,

I am in receipt of yours of the 27th inst. Many thanks for the wine gums. You were right they did make me feel better.

Good news! Father Gibney has talked Dermot into taking an English course here in the prison. This is the first course he has taken since we got in here. He is at last beginning to settle down. I am going to join the class too.

Thank you for Cathys address. I have already written a letter to her so I hope she writes back. I couldnt remember her daughters name so I just put the baby. I hope she doesnt mind. Best wishes to everyone and Pierre.

Yours sincerely,
Buster Brady.

Chapter 15

'YOU CAN TELL HIM TO GO AND SHITE,' Sue White roared in from the other room. She had picked this phrase up from Trevor. The word 'shite' doesn't sound the same when said with an English accent though.

'Can you hear her?' Trevor spoke in a low tone into the mouthpiece of the 'phone. It was Tony on the other end of the line.

The row had started over nothing, it seemed. Well, not exactly nothing, it was a small sculpture actually. It's title was 'Dreaming Wolf', although Dermot thought it looked more like 'Sleeping Red Setter'. What it looked like wasn't important, the row had erupted over what it had cost: three hundred pounds. Sue had seen it, she had liked it, so she bought it. Tony went ballistic. A screaming match had followed with both sides using the usual ammunition – words like 'irresponsible', 'stingy', 'childish'. The row culminated in Tony's screamed promise that he was 'walking out that door and never coming back', and finally the slamming of the door. This was followed by some very loud crying and smashing of ornaments against the wall.

When the crashing and banging died down and the crying was reduced to just a soft whimper, Trevor felt it was safe to come out of his bedroom. He made Sue a cup of coffee and tried to console her as best he could. That had been three hours ago. Sue had stopped crying now, but was still angry. Tony told Trevor that he had only called to see that Sue was all right. He had no intention, he reiterated, of returning. Trevor spoke again into the mouthpiece of the 'phone. 'Look, Tony, you stay in that hotel tonight, I'll call you first thing in the morning, okay? Good night.' He hung up the phone and returned to the room.

'So what did Scrooge have to say for himself?' Sue asked, full of drama.

'He's going to stay in a hotel tonight.'

'A hotel? Ha! No, Trevor, he'll probably sleep in a cardboard box in Piccadilly Circus! Not a hotel, not our Tony. Hotels cost fucking money!'

'You don't think you're being a bit hard on him, Sue?'

Sue turned on Trevor. 'No, I don't think I'm being hard on him, Trevor. He's a tight-fisted bastard, he doesn't want me to spend any money because he doesn't want me to have a good time. He wants to sit in. He wants to save. He wants to be careful.'

'He wants to get married, Sue,' Trevor said very evenly.

Sue stopped in her tracks. She ran her hand through her hair and slowly sat down and lit a cigarette.

Trevor sat down beside her and began to speak softly. 'He wants a nice wedding reception, he wants a semi-detached house in Surrey, he wants two cars, he wants all of that for you and him, and he knows that that takes money.'

Sue's hand shook as she put the cigarette to her lips. When she had digested Trevor's words she suddenly stood up and turned her back to him.

'Well, he can go and shite,' she said defiantly.

'Don't do this, Sue.'

'Do what?'

'Don't throw it all down the toilet. He loves you.'

Sue didn't reply, nor did she turn around. So Trevor spoke to her back. 'The two of you are going to blow probably the finest relationship I have ever seen and all because you're both too stupid to recognise how much you love each other.'

Sue slowly turned and looked at Trevor. He wasn't finished – he was on a roll now. 'Believe me, Sue, I know this. The opportunity of real love comes along very, very rarely and when it does you have to grasp it with both hands. If you don't ...' Trevor now sat down slowly. He wasn't looking at Sue, he wasn't even talking to Sue. 'If you don't, you will regret it for the rest of your life.' Trevor looked up at Sue. 'I know this, Sue!'

Sue could tell from Trevor's face that he did know it. She stubbed out her cigarette and picked up the two mugs from the coffee table. 'I'll make us another cup of coffee, shall I, Trevor?' Without waiting for an answer she left the room.

Ten minutes later she returned with two hot mugs of coffee. When she was seated, Trevor asked, 'Are you okay?'

Sue simply nodded. She lit another cigarette and it became obvious the way she settled herself in the chair that she was ready to talk. 'You're right, Trevor.'

'I know I am.'

'And you're not the first to tell me that. You know Nicky in Glasgow?'

'Yes I do, what about her?'

101

'She said the same thing to me two years ago. Do you know, Trevor, when she was in college some guy used to leave little paintings for her. Tiny little copies of some of the great works of art. She'd find them in weird places, Trevor, and the first letter of the artist's name corresponded with a letter in her name. She never found out who it was, and she tells me she regrets it to this day. You're right, Trevor, this is make-or-break for me and Tony, either we get married or we finish it now.'

Sue wasn't looking at Trevor during the telling of any of this story. Trevor, on the other hand, was transfixed, eating every word that came out of her mouth. The blood had drained from his face, he felt dizzy, his mouth had gone completely dry, and when the question came he could barely get the words out of his mouth.

'Nicky? In Glasgow – Nicky?'

Sue now noticed the change in Trevor. 'Yes, what about her?'

'What's her surname? What's Nicky's surname?'

'That is her surname, Trevor. Well, that's not all of her surname, her surname is Nicholson – she's Maria Nicholson – but everybody calls her Nicky.'

* * *

The four of them sat around the circular table in the dining room of the house in Cookham. It was Tony Vescoli's first night back in the house since his departure four days earlier. At the same time as Trevor had gone to the hotel to pick Tony up, Sue had gone to the station to meet Maria Nicholson. Sue was delighted when Trevor asked her to invite Nicky down for the dinner. For two reasons: firstly she would at last get a chance to introduce her two 'Cupid' failures to each other, and secondly it would help to break the ice on Tony's return.

When Trevor arrived at the hotel it was hard to tell which of the two men was the more nervous. When Tony opened the door of the hotel room he had his shirt collar turned up and a tie wrapped awkwardly around it.

'I can't tie this, Trevor, my hands are shaking so much,' Tony said.

'Well, don't fucking ask me, Tony,' Trevor replied.

'Jesus Christ, Trevor, you'd think it was your big night and not mine.' Tony laughed, but it was a nervous laugh.

But now here they all sat, at the table in a circle. Tony facing Sue, Trevor facing Nicky. If Nicky recognised Trevor, she showed no flicker of it in her expression. Her greeting when introduced to Trevor had been very formal and her thoughts seemed to be all on how the evening would turn out for Tony and Sue. Sue had obviously filled Nicky in on the situation, between phone calls and on the journey from the train station. Sue, with a little help from Nicky, had prepared a beautiful meal of stuffed pork fillets, broccoli, asparagus and new potatoes, to be fol-lowed by lemon cheesecake with cream – all of which, coincidentally, happened to be Tony's favourite dishes. The table had been cleared of all the used dishes by now and held only four coffee cups, a coffee pot, sugar bowl, cream jug, three empty wine bottles and a candelabra. Tony coughed, ready to make his announcement.

'Susan White, begging your indulgence and that of our esteemed company,' he nodded towards Trevor and Nicky, and they both nodded back, 'I would like to formally ask you to be my wife. If you accept, I would ask you –' and now Tony put his hand into his jacket pocket and produced a small, purple, velvet-coated box. He opened the box to reveal a beautiful three-stone engagement ring, '– to wear this ring as a sign of our engagement.'

The proposal was very formal, although Trevor expected nothing less from Tony. Sue stared at the ring for some moments before she removed it from the box. Slowly she slid it on her wedding finger and looked up at Tony with a beaming smile on her face. 'I love you Tony Vescoli.'

'I love you too, Sue White.'

As Tony and Sue kissed, Trevor and Nicky clapped.

'This calls for champagne,' exclaimed Trevor. He left the room to collect the bottle of champagne from the fridge. When he returned and all the glasses were filled, the four of them toasted the happy couple.

The toast completed, Trevor cleared his throat. 'I feel it would be a terrible travesty to have two beautiful women at a table and have gifts for only one,' he announced. The two women giggled like little girls.

'Well, good on you, Trevor,' Tony said, and he slapped Trevor on the back.

Trevor reached into his back pocket and extracted his wallet. He carefully placed the wallet on the table and opened it flat. The eyes of the other three were riveted on the wallet. Slowly, from the back of his wallet, Trevor slid out the last canvas from the Maria Nicholson collection. He placed it in front of Nicky. Then he spoke the words that he had rehearsed with Rory and Dino, that had been stuck in his throat for so many years: 'Add this to your collection, Maria!'

*   *   *

Trevor Browne and Maria Nicholson were married twelve weeks later in a small Catholic church in Deepcut in Surrey. The only two of the Browne family who were not at the ceremony were Trevor's brother Dermot and his sister Cathy. Although she enjoyed the day enormously, Trevor's mother, Agnes, was dismayed that yet again a family celebration had come and gone and she had failed to gather all of her family into one room.

Chapter 16

CATHY WAS DELIGHTED when she recieved Buster's letter. It had been a long time since anyone, either in the written word or verbally, had asked her how she was. Buster had also used phrases like 'I hope you are as beautiful as ever', which made her feel like a teenager once again. She read his letter at the breakfast table, alone. Mick had not returned home from his late shift. Again. She read it to herself first, then she read it aloud to Pamela. Cathy's baby daughter smiled and gurgled in the right places, and when Cathy finished reading, Pamela frowned and began to cry, so Cathy read it again, and again. Until eventually Pamela drifted off to sleep with Buster Brady's words ringing in her ears.

Pamela's birth had made no difference at all to Cathy's relationship with Mick. Cathy no longer fooled herself that she was in a real marriage or that Mick would ever be anything other than the bastard he was. But where could she go? What could she do? It had certainly crossed her mind on some days to just pack up everything and move herself and Pamela back to Dublin to her mother's. But then she would recall her best friend Cathy Dowdall and the harrowing years she had had in her late teens trying to support herself and her child alone. So the thought of leaving would quickly vanish from her mind. Instead she kept a good home and poured all of her energies and attention into Pamela. While Pamela was sleeping, Cathy tidied the kitchen and then sat down at the table and replied to Buster's letter. She began to tell Buster of the state of affairs between herself and Mick. It was the first time she had ever told anyone what was going on and when the letter was posted she felt strangely lighter. Cathy O'Leary knew she was trapped. She knew she couldn't change Mick O'Leary. She knew she couldn't change circumstances. She knew the first thing that had to change was Cathy O'Leary and with an infant child she wasn't ready for that change. Not yet.

*   *   *

The C-block supervisor gave permission for Dermot to walk Buster down to the administration building. It was March 24th, Buster's release day. They strolled together slowly towards the building, Buster carrying a nylon bag containing the meagre belongings he was taking home with him. Dermot walked by his side, his hands in his pockets. When they reached the door of the admin. building, and Dermot could go no farther, they stopped. The two men turned to face each other. Dermot looked down on his chubby little best friend. He was about to speak when the admin. door opened and the new arrivals for the day were bustled through. Dermot and Buster looked at the new boys arriving.

'Same old faces, they just keep coming back,' Dermot said flatly.

'Yeh. But it won't be me, Dermo. I'm never coming back.'

They looked at each other again.

'I hope not, Buster. Look, when I get out of here ...' Dermot began. 'Well, yeh know.' Dermot began to shuffle his feet.

'Dermo, I'll be outside that gate waiting for yeh. I will!' Buster's eyes were filling up.

'Sure, don't I know you will, Buster,' Dermot slapped Buster on the shoulder. 'Now, go on, get the hell out of here.' Dermot turned and began to walk away.

'Dermo?' Buster called.

Dermot turned.

'Can I write to you?' Buster asked.

'You'd better or I'll kill you when I get out,' Dermot replied with a smile. The two men burst into that laughter of sadness that only parting friends can know.

That evening as he queued for his food in Mountjoy Prison, Dermot wasn't in the humour for conversation, but he had little choice. One of the new arrivals recognised him. Dermot wanted to tell him to shut the fuck up and allow him to just pick up his food and get back to his cell to eat his dinner in peace. But Dermot also knew that feeling of 'just in' and how sometimes the only way to relieve the nerves was to talk and talk. So he let the man go on. Little of what the guy was saying was of any interest to Dermot but he feigned attention. Until the man said, 'Oh yeh, by the way an old friend of yours croaked it!'

This got Dermot's interest. 'Croaked it? Died, like?'

'Yeh, overdosed on heroin!' The man now spoke with the relish a gossip has in the knowledge that he is imparting fresh news.

'A friend of mine? Who?'

'Your woman from Townsend Street. What's her name? Eh ... Mary Carter! Yeh, that's it, Mary Carter.'

Dermot instantly dropped his tray. He pushed the man aside, turned around and began to make his way unsteadily back to his cell. As he reached the top of the stairs of his own landing he threw up. Father Gibney spent that night with Dermot in his cell, the young prison chaplain listening through massive sobs to the outpourings of guilt and regret from a broken young man.

PART TWO

Chapter 17

BECAUSE ST CHRISTOPHER'S NATIONAL SCHOOL was smack in the middle of the city centre the high railing that surrounded the play yard was essential. This kept the children from straying from the school and onto the busy city streets. Needless to say, the older boys, those of ten or twelve years of age, had found ways to scamper either over or through the railings and make their way to the local shops when the teachers weren't looking. However, the railings kept the younger boys in. It was the morning break and children were screaming and running in all directions all over the school yard. The chatter of their voices was deafening. At one end of the yard was a long stone building with a long bench along the wall; the children referred to this as 'the shelter'. They would sit on the bench and eat their sandwiches or drink their milk, or whatever they had.

Cormac Carter cupped his hands together and blew hard into them. For a fraction of a second they warmed and then went cold again. It was freezing. He repeated the action three or four times before pulling his hands apart and sliding them up the sleeves of his duffle coat. This is how his Aunt Margaret taught him to warm his hands. Cormac lived with his aunt in one of the new inner city houses built in The Jarro. Aunt Margaret had five other children, and they all got to call her 'Mammy'. Cormac had to call her Aunt Margaret. Cormac did not have a Mammy. He once had had a Mammy, Aunt Margaret told him, but he could not remember her. Aunt Margaret said she had died. Cormac didn't really understand 'died'.

With his hands warm, he leaned against the end wall of the shelter and slowly inched his face out until just his eye was looking out from the school yard. The eye wandered for a little and then focused on its target. He was here again. Cormac quickly pulled his head back. He wondered who this person was, this man who had been hanging around the school every day at playtime for the last few weeks. He had told Aunt Margaret about him at tea one evening. She had quickly looked over at Uncle John who was reading his newspaper. Uncle John looked up from the paper to meet her gaze. He shrugged and went back to his paper. Aunt Margaret had simply said, 'Don't mind him.'

Cormac took another peep out at the man. I wonder who he is, thought the boy. He made a decision there and then. Puffing up his chest he stepped out of the shelter and began to walk across the yard towards the man. He was going to ask this man who he was. He did not get the chance. The man saw him coming and by the time Cormac had got halfway across the school yard the man had vanished. The little six-year-old stood with his hands on his hips wondering.

110

'Jesus, that was close,' Dermot said aloud. His words were punctuated by puffs of steam as his warm breath met the icy air. He would have to give this up now. He was six weeks out of prison and every weekday for the last four weeks he had come to the school. It had taken just one day and a couple of questions to some of the older children to find out which one was Cormac Carter. He had watched him every day since, as if hoping in some way that in a gesture or a movement Cormac would confirm to Dermot that he was indeed his son. He hadn't seen anything. He knew Cormac was living with Margaret Carter – a bitch, but good with kids. She was Mary's eldest sister. Dermot heard the bells of St Jarlath's church ringing out the twelve o'clock Angelus, and again he spoke aloud to himself, 'Christ, I have to get to work.' He checked his plastic bag to make sure it hadn't burst. Then he quickly headed off down the street.

Since his release from prison, Dermot had been staying in the Iveagh Hostel near Christchurch in Dublin. It was Father Gibney who found him the accommodation, although he tried first to talk Dermot into going back to live with his mother. Dermot wouldn't hear of it. He knew he had changed a lot himself over his six and a half years in prison. But the bitter memory of that confrontation with his mother in the visiting room of Mountjoy Prison had not left him. His feelings about that hadn't changed.

The Iveagh Hostel was a shelter for indigent men. It had originally been set up and donated to Dublin city by Lord and Lady Iveagh of the Guinness family, and was now run by volunteers. It was crowded at night, and noisy too. A lot of the men staying there had drink or psychiatric problems. There were no cooking facilities, though you

got a cup of tea every morning before you left at 8am.
Dermot didn't have to worry about his meals during the
day, for Father Gibney had also fixed him up with a job.
The priest had explained to Dermot that the job didn't
pay too much but at least it was a start, and if he was wise
and put a few pounds aside he could eventually move
into a flat and get himself a better job. When Father
Gibney told Dermot of the position he was being offered
Dermot smiled wryly. Dermot was now a kitchen porter
in the Gresham Hotel, just like his father had been twenty
years previously. Maybe his mother was right, maybe he
was just like his father. Anyway, although the money
wasn't great, thanks to the Iveagh Hostel Dermot was able
to save a few pounds, and thanks to the Gresham Hotel
– for Dermot had all his meals there – he had put on
weight since leaving prison.

When he arrived at the Gresham Hotel that day he went
to the locker room. He changed into his kitchen overalls
and, carefully placing his plastic bag of books in the
bottom of his locker, he closed and locked it. For the next
eight hours Dermot would wash pots.

Chapter 18

NO MATTER WHAT WAY TREVOR JUGGLED the figures around, once he added them up it made for depressing reading. There was no escaping the harsh reality – Nicholson Books Limited was in big trouble. It was going to be a bleak Christmas for the company's two directors and sole shareholders, Trevor and Maria Browne. They had founded the company just two years previously. It was an idea Maria had had for a long time, to publish a selection of children's books containing the highest standard of illustration. They had certainly achieved this – everyone agreed that the illustrations in Nicholson books were among the finest in the United Kingdom. But despite this, the books weren't selling. Their first three publications – *King Benny, Lady Esther's Adventure* and *Jenny and Jane* – had done reasonably well and even turned a little profit. However, they were followed by six very mediocre books. The last two that they had published, *Louis the Lawnmower* and *Pauly's Folly,* were unmitigated disasters.

Trevor sighed heavily as he put his pen down. He removed his glasses and began to massage the bridge of his nose just as Maria arrived into the room with coffee and biscuits. She placed the tray on the table and then wrapped her arms around Trevor from behind. He smiled.

It was one of Maria's greatest talents, delivering a hug just when it was needed.

'Is it that bad?' she asked as she passed him his coffee.

'Yes, it's that bad!' he answered. 'We've a printing bill for three and a half thousand pounds, we're two months behind in the payments for the car, we're probably going to have the 'phone cut off, and we still owe Hobson's over a thousand pounds for those cardboard display boxes we got for *Henry Hippo*. Christ, they were a waste!' Trevor threw down the pen again.

'No, they weren't a waste, Trevor. They were a good idea. And we certainly can't blame them for *Henry Hippo*'s failure. It was just a shit book!' This statement brought a sideways glance from Trevor. *He* had illustrated *Henry Hippo*. Maria caught his glance and was quick to add, 'The illustrations were fine, it was just a weak story. How are this month's sales?'

Trevor riffled through the pages on the table-top until he came across the sales results sheet. He began to run down the titles with his finger.

'Well, *Lady Esther* and *King Benny* are starting to move a bit, they should sell well over the Christmas. It's hard to know how these four –' he ran his finger over the page, 'will go, but we can expect seventy-five percent of *Pauly*, and probably all of *Henry Hippo* to be returned.'

'Christ, it is looking bad, isn't it, Trevor?'

'Yes, it is.' The couple began to sip their coffee, and they both sank into silent contemplation. Trevor stood up from the table and walked to the fireplace. He lifted the tongs and placed a few more pieces of coal on the open fire. A small Christmas tree glittered in the corner, the tinsel shivering in the heat haze that oozed from the fireplace.

'If only we could attract some of the really big writers, like Keith Clarke or Wilbur Livingston,' Trevor exclaimed.

'But that takes money, Trevor. We don't have enough to pay our own bills, never mind give big-name writers big advances.'

'You're right,' Trevor replied in a resigned tone and returned to his coffee.

'I spoke to Sue today,' Maria announced and she brightened as she always did when Sue's name was mentioned.

Trevor also brightened. 'Did you? And how are things in the advertising world?'

Tony and Sue had moved to Liverpool where they too were pursuing their dream. They had opened up a small advertising agency of their own. At last count the Vescoli White Agency had twenty solid clients on its books. The business had grown from working from home to a large five-roomed office complex in Liverpool city centre. Tony was very proud of the fact that they had made a go of the agency without taking one single account with them from Hutchinson & Bailey. Not the usual practice in the advertising world.

'Sue says business is quiet, although it always is at this time of the year,' Maria answered. Maria paused, taking extra care about how she phrased her next sentence; her husband was a proud man. 'Sue says ... that she and Tony could do with some help in the New Year ... if we're not bogged down by work ourselves. What do you think?'

Trevor saw through it straight away, but he wasn't angry. 'I know they mean well, love, but we really have to make a definite decision. Either we go on trying to make a go of this or we go back into advertising on a full-time basis. Don't you agree? A handout from Tony and Sue, well-meaning or not, is still a handout and it will only solve our problems in the short term. I must ring them tomorrow and thank them.'

'So, when do you think we should make this decision, then?'

'Well – I think it would be foolish to make any decision till we see how the Christmas sales go. We'll leave things sit over the Christmas period and maybe by mid-January the picture will be clearer. Let's make our decision then. If we decide to go back into advertising full-time, it may mean moving out of here and back to London,' Trevor said with a little woe in his voice.

Maria let out a sigh; she liked this house. She liked the area too. When they had decided to go into children's book publishing they had also decided to move away from London. It was Maria who found the house they were now renting in Altringham, just on the outskirts of Manchester. She hated the thought of moving out of this house nearly as much as she dreaded the thought of moving back to London.

Chapter 19

PIERRE OPENED THE FRONT DOOR of 43 Wolfe Tone Grove. Agnes Browne stood before him in a dreadful state. Her hair was ragged and dripping wet from the rain, her coat was soaked and covered in mud all down one side. Her wool-lined suede boots were covered in so much mud that you couldn't see the zippers.

'My God, what has happened to you?' Pierre exclaimed.

'I fell. Get out of the way,' Agnes said, disgruntled, as she pushed past Pierre.

'Where were you?' Pierre asked, concerned.

'Out!' Agnes snapped as she made her way to the bathroom, kicking her boots off on the way. Within fifteen minutes Agnes was immersed in a steaming hot bath. Pierre had taken her boots out to the back yard where he scraped all the mud off and left them in the coal shed to dry. He went back into the kitchen, put on the kettle and while he waited for it to boil, he gathered up Agnes's wet clothes and hung them in the hot press to dry. He then brought Agnes in a cup of steaming hot tea and sat down on the toilet bowl.

'You were out looking for Dermot again, weren't you?' Pierre asked.

Agnes lay in the bath, her eyes closed, the scent of Radox gently tickling her nose. She didn't answer.

'You know, Agnes, my love, Dermot has a lot of things to get right in his mind before he even dreams of mending fences. Six and a half years is a long time to be locked away, Agnes. Things that you and I take for granted, Dermot must learn all over again. Simple things like crossing the road. And big things like how to become part of society again, how to deal with people, how to deal with pain. When he's ready he will come,' Pierre finished.

Agnes didn't move. Her eyes didn't open nor did her expression change. 'Pierre, leave me alone, please.' Agnes's voice was tired.

Pierre left the bathroom and returned to his armchair by the fire, where he continued to wrap the Christmas presents for Agnes's grandchildren.

*   *   *

All along Dame Street in Dublin's city centre, people were scurrying this way and that in an effort to stay out of the rain. The film of rainwater on the ground made the streets look black at night and they reflected the city lights. In virtually every shop doorway along Dame Street people were sheltering. Not Dermot Browne however. He walked along the street with the footpath virtually to himself and a smile on his face. He loved the feel of the rain. In prison he had missed the rain. If it were raining, the inmates were not allowed out into the exercise yard, so for six and a half years Dermot Browne hadn't felt the rain on his face. To Dermot the ice-cold rain dripping from his face was a symbol of freedom.

He had just finished a ten-hour day at the Gresham Hotel. The hotel was at its busiest during the Christmas weeks, with dinner dances and Christmas parties. He liked working overtime. He'd little else to do. When he arrived at the Iveagh Hostel, dripping wet, he was met in the hallway by one of the volunteers with a cup of hot tea. He then went to his cot, on the end of which he hung his wet clothes. The hostel was noisy and overcrowded, but it was warm. He propped his pillow up against the headboard of his bed and sat cross-legged on the bed. He lifted his nylon bag from the floor and took out his books.

The English course he had taken in prison had encouraged an interest in reading. He was a fussy reader and preferred children's or teenage books to adult books. Adult books, he thought, were too complicated and many of them were too sad to read in prison. So instead he had taken to books aimed at a younger audience and he devoured everything that they had in the library. He had been stunned one day to find a book called *Lady Esther's Adventure* in the children's section – stunned because it bore the name of Trevor Browne as author and illustrator. Just a quick flick through the illustrations confirmed to Dermot that his brother was now writing and illustrating books. He glowed with pride. He also stole the book. He then wrote a letter to Trevor at the publisher's address given in the book, telling him how proud he was of him, and was delighted within weeks to receive a package containing seven more books. But he had to admit that although the illustrations were beautiful the stories were crap. Nevertheless, his youngest brother was an author and publisher, and Dermot was very proud of that. He flicked through the pages of *Lady Esther's Adventure* once again. He wondered what young Cormac would think if he knew that he had an uncle who was an author and illustrator. He wondered if young Cormac knew that he had an uncle.

Trevor was the first person that Dermot had 'phoned on his release from prison. He rang Trevor at his home in Manchester to thank him. Just a week before Dermot's release day he had received a letter from Trevor containing fifty pounds, which Trevor had sent to help Dermot in his first days of freedom. Things must be good in the book world, Dermot thought. Over the following couple of weeks Dermot contacted all of his family. Except his mother. He'd had a varying reaction from each of them, but they all wanted to help him. He was glad of that but refused all their offers as he knew the next few steps had to be taken alone.

When he called in to Mark's office at Senga Furnishings, Mark's initial welcome had been warm, with a big hug for his brother. Then, over a cup of coffee, Mark offered him a job in Senga where now, by the way, Buster Brady was also working. But Mark had insisted that before he could take Dermot on, he would have to make up with his mother. Dermot told Mark that what was between his mother and him was his business and none of Mark's affair. Mark then kicked into his fatherly mode and the whole thing degenerated into a row. Dermot marched out of the offices with Mark shouting 'Selfish bastard!' after him.

Rory and Dino were delighted to see Dermot. Dino styled Dermot's hair while Rory filled Dermot in on all the family news. He went back to their apartment on Appian Way in Donnybrook for dinner that evening. Before he left them, Rory and Dino offered Dermot some clothes to wear until he got himself 'fixed up'. Dermot was thankful for the offer and knew it was genuine – but he wasn't sure what kind of reaction he would get in the Iveagh Hostel if he arrived in skin-tight denim jeans and a cerise chiffon blouse, so he declined.

He hadn't been down to Arklow to see Cathy. When he 'phoned her she had asked him not to come, as a visit from an ex-prisoner might 'unsettle' Mick. At Simon's house in Raheny, Dermot was made feel very welcome and he actually stayed the weekend there. Young Thomas was around the same age as Cormac, and was a real character. He really took to his Uncle Dermot, and the feeling was decidedly mutual. Over the weeks, Dermot had met up with Buster on a few occasions to have a couple of drinks. Buster was living with his eldest sister Sharon, out in Ballyfermot. Buster told Dermot he was getting on well in Senga Furnishings and had started saving in a building society account in the hopes of some day getting a mortgage to own his own house. Buster Brady owning his own house, what was the world coming to? Dermot smiled to himself as he sat on the bed in the Iveagh Hostel. He returned *Lady Esther's Adventure* to the bag and took out one of his Biggles books, which he read till he fell asleep.

Chapter 20

IT HAD NOW VIRTUALLY BECOME A TRADITION. On Christmas Day all of the Browne family who were Dublin-based would come to Mark and Betty's house for tea. Everybody would make their own arrangements for Christmas dinner, but by early evening Agnes Browne's children and grandchildren would be sitting in Mark's house exchanging Christmas gifts. Agnes's arrangements for Christmas dinner changed every year as she shuttled between each member of the family. This Christmas she and Pierre were to have Christmas dinner in Raheny with Simon, Fiona and Thomas. The five of them would then drive out to Mark's house for tea.

Rory would join Dino's family for dinner. The Doyles were well aware that their son, Dino, was homosexual, and were delighted that he had found a stable partner in Rory. Rory was welcomed into the Doyle home as if he were a son. Dermot had declined an offer of Christmas dinner at Simon's, because his mother would be there. He'd also declined the evening party at Mark's for the same reason. Instead, Dermot joined hordes of Dublin's homeless at the Mansion House in Dawson Street where he enjoyed a slap-up Christmas dinner and a few glasses of wine with the compliments of Dublin's Lord Mayor. He left the Mansion House around 7pm on Christmas night, a little tipsy. He didn't want to go straight back to the Iveagh Hostel so instead he walked the streets of Dublin.

In Arklow, Cathy O'Leary was enjoying her best Christmas since the day she was married. She had made the excuse to her husband that Pamela was too ill for the long drive to Cork. Undeterred, as soon as Christmas dinner was finished, Mick loaded gifts for his parents into the car and took off alone for Cork, where he would stay for the next three days. Thanks to his departure, Cathy was having something on Christmas night that she had not had for many years. Sex! Pamela was asleep in her cot in the other room, after a wonderful day. And now Cathy, smelling of Chanel No. 5, a gift from her lover, was kneeling naked on her double bed. She was bent over her exhausted, sleeping lover, her long black hair sweeping across his stomach. She gently rolled her tongue around his nipple and even in his sleep he smiled in recognition of the pleasurable sensation. Fuck you, Mick O'Leary, was Cathy's thought as she snuggled into her lover's arms.

At nine-thirty, Agnes made the excuse to her family that she was feeling tired and that Pierre was going to drive her home. After lots of hugs and kisses, she and Pierre pulled away from Mark's house. When they reached the crossroads at the Oscar Traynor Road, where Pierre would usually turn right and head for Finglas, Agnes instructed him to drive straight on and into the city centre. She had an errand to run. Fifteen minutes later, Pierre's car pulled up outside 26 Michael Collins Court in The Jarro. Pierre unlocked the boot of the car and gave Agnes a box wrapped in Christmas paper. As Agnes made her way to the front door, Pierre sat back in the car and waited. The door was opened after the second knock. Margaret O'Brien, Mary Carter's eldest sister, was a little startled to see Mrs Browne standing at the front door with the Christmas gift for Cormac.

'I'm sorry to disturb you on Christmas night, love ... this is just something for Cormac.' Agnes proffered the gift.

Instead of taking the box from Agnes's hands, Margaret stood back and held the door open. 'Step in for a minute, Mrs Browne, won't you?'

Agnes stood into the hallway and Margaret closed the door. 'Maybe you'd like to give it to him yourself, Mrs Browne?'

'God no, eh ... you give it to him, love. It'll just confuse him, he'll wonder who I am. It's just a little something, eh, that Dermot sent for him.'

'And why didn't Dermot deliver it himself, Mrs Browne?'

'Oh he's away, on business,' Agnes lied.

'I don't think so, Mrs Browne. He's actually standing in a doorway across the street.'

*   *   *

After walking up and down across the street from 26 Michael Collins Court for an hour Dermot had begun to think he was going mad. 'What the fuck am I doing?' he asked himself aloud. He stood into a doorway directly across the road from the house. From where he stood Dermot could see a crack of light come through the side window of number twenty-six, where the curtain was slightly parted. If I could sneak over there I could probably peek in through the crack and see the boy, he thought. He left the doorway and walked to the edge of the kerb, but suddenly heard a car coming down the street. He turned quickly and stepped back into the shadow of the doorway. He would wait till the car had passed. But it didn't pass; instead it pulled up outside number twenty-six. Dermot recognised the driver. It was Pierre.

'What the fuck are they doing here?' Dermot exclaimed.

When Dermot saw his mother step from the car, his eyes filled up and he began to gag a little. He watched as Agnes and Pierre went to the boot of the car and took out a large box covered in Christmas wrapping paper. He watched from the shadows as Margaret O'Brien held the door wide open; then Agnes stepped through the doorway and the door closed. Twenty minutes later Agnes emerged from the house, and she exchanged words with Margaret O'Brien before the door closed once more. Agnes then got into the car, and she and Pierre talked for a few seconds before Pierre gunned the engine and the car disappeared around the corner. Dermot waited for five minutes. The street had now become totally quiet and it had begun to snow. He left his hiding place in the doorway and quickly walked across the street through the flurry of crystal white snow. Instead of going in the gateway of number twenty-six he went instead in the gateway of number twenty-eight. He walked up to the door as if he were going to knock on it, glanced quickly around to see that nobody was there, then vaulted the fence into twenty-six and pressed himself flat against the side wall. Crouching, he made his way to the side window and slowly rose till his eyes were level with the crack in the curtain.

The room seemed to be full of children. But he easily picked out the boy, the only blonde among them. Cormac was sitting directly beneath the Christmas tree, on the floor. He was in the process of removing the Christmas wrapping from the box that Agnes had delivered. With the wrapping paper gone, he then tore the cardboard box itself to shreds, eventually extracting a shiny red fire truck. Suddenly David, one of Margaret O'Brien's children and two years older than Cormac, walked over to where Cormac was sitting. Dermot couldn't hear what was being said but it was obvious that the older boy wanted the fire truck and just as obvious that Cormac wasn't parting with it. The older boy made to snatch the truck from Cormac, but Cormac held on. Cormac stood up and the truck now became the subject of a tug-of-war between the two boys. Cormac was strong for six years of age, and holding on to the truck with one hand he swung the other arm around, catching David with a full-fisted blow to the cheek. David released his grip on the fire truck and left the room in tears. Having won the battle of the truck, Cormac then did a strange thing. Instead of retreating to his previous sitting position and playing with the truck he walked to the side of the fireplace where Martin O'Brien, another of Margaret's children but this time three years younger than Cormac, was sitting. Cormac presented Martin with the truck. The two children smiled at each other and Martin began to lick the truck.

'Now *that's* my fuckin' kid,' Dermot exclaimed.

Despite the freezing cold, and the falling snow, Dermot Browne hadn't felt as warm in a long, long time. He vaulted the fence onto the street and briskly made his way back to the Iveagh Hostel.

* * *

When Dermot had left the street, the shadowy figure of a woman emerged from the doorway that Dermot had been using earlier as a hiding place. Quickly the woman scurried around the corner and vanished from view. Within seconds a car engine could be heard starting, a car door slammed and the sound vanished into the night. Agnes Browne considered that the first sighting she had had of her son Dermot in nearly six years was the finest Christmas present she had received that year. When they returned to Wolfe Tone Grove, Pierre du Gloss received his nicest Christmas present too. No clothes pegs were necessary.

* * *

In Trevor's house in Altringham everybody was very cosy. Sue and Tony had arrived there at about 8pm and when the snow started to fall they decided to stay overnight. By midnight Nicky and Sue were in night clothes drinking eggnogs, and Trevor and Tony were three-quarters of the way through a bottle of brandy.

'So, from what you're saying,' Tony began, as he poured himself another brandy into the snifter, 'nothing short of a miracle will save the company?' Tony wasn't being malicious, but the two couples were friendly enough to be able to discuss these matters without having to beat around the bush.

'That's about the size of it,' Trevor said, his speech slightly slurred. Tony sat down beside Trevor again and clinked his glass against Trevor's glass.

'Well, Trevor my son, miracles *do* happen!' Tony smiled and Sue chirped in, 'Yes, they do ... especially at Christmas.'

And as the snow gently and quietly laid a blanket across Altringham the four toasted each other's health.

*   *   *

It is the tradition in Dublin that all pubs close on St Stephen's Day, 26 December. However, if one is in the know, one can always find a pub that's open. When Dermot tapped with a coin on the window of Foley's lounge bar in The Jarro he wasn't sure what kind of reception to expect. He needn't have worried. Mr Foley welcomed him with open arms and, indeed, stood him his first pint. Over the drinks that followed, Dermot told Mr Foley of all that had happened since that night nearly seven years ago when he and Buster had left Foley's bar and stolen the bus. By the time Dermot reached the part of the story where he admitted to Mr Foley that Cormac was indeed his son, he had had about fourteen pints.

'And I'm going to get him, Mr Foley, I am. I'm going to take him to live with me,' Dermot announced this last part to the whole bar. 'What do you think, Mr Foley?' Dermot asked.

'I think, Dermot, you should have a bit of dinner and a cup of tea. Come on inside.' Mr Foley lifted the flap at the bar and Dermot made his way unsteadily into the back room. After he had downed two cups of coffee, Monica Foley placed a plate of dinner in front of Dermot that was big enough to feed an army. When the meal was finished and Mr Foley had brought him another cup of coffee, Dermot felt a lot better. A little less drunk, but not entirely sober. He was grateful for the Foleys' hospitality.

'I meant it, Mr Foley,' Dermot suddenly said.

'What's that, Dermot?'

'The boy, I'm gonna have the boy live with me. And I'll be a good father too.'

'Of course you will, Dermot, now why don't you sit over here in the armchair beside the fire and have a little sleep, eh ... it will do you good.' Mr Foley puffed up the cushions on the chair and Dermot relaxed into it and within minutes was asleep. When he woke an hour later he was drenched in perspiration and the side of his face was scarlet red from the heat of the fire.

'Jesus Christ, I'm burnin'.' Dermot stood up a little unsteadily. There was nobody else in the back room; both Mr and Mrs Foley were out in the bar, serving. Dermot made his way to the toilet, relieved himself and then went out to the lounge to where the Foleys were. Monica Foley greeted him. 'Ah there you are, Dermot. Are you feeling better, ready for another session?'

Dermot smiled, but dismissed the suggestion of another session with a wave of his hand.

'God no, Monica. Listen, I'm off. Tell Mr Foley thanks very much and a very happy new year to both of you.' Dermot banged his head climbing under the flap of the bar and seconds later he was standing outside in the snow-covered street. He had a feeling that he had something to do; he couldn't remember what it was, but he knew he had *something* to do. Then it dawned on him. Five minutes later he was knocking on the door of 26

Michael Collins Court. Margaret O'Brien opened the door and Dermot enjoyed the look of surprise on her face.

'What do *you* want?' She made it sound like an accusation rather than a question.

'I want the boy,' Dermot declared.

'Which boy would that be now? I have four of them,' Margaret O'Brien said sarcastically.

'My boy, me son!'

'Oh, he's *your* son now, is he?'

'He was *always* me son, and I want him.'

'You just wait there now, Dermot Browne.' Margaret O'Brien closed the door. Dermot had been expecting this. She was gone to get John, her husband. Dermot knew John O'Brien – he wasn't a bad sort, decent lad, but if he had to, Dermot would beat the crap out of him. Dermot rolled his sleeves up to his elbows and awaited his opponent. Fifteen minutes later he heard the latch begin to turn. He stood back from the door and struck a John L Sullivan pose. When the door opened Dermot's opponent was a lot smaller than he had expected. Slowly Dermot lowered his fists. Cormac stood in the doorway, with a puzzled look on his face. He was wearing his grey duffle coat. In his right hand he had a small cardboard suitcase, and under his left arm he held a shiny red fire truck. Margaret O'Brien gave the boy a little push out of the doorway.

'Now, Mr Big Shite, take your son. I've enough of me own. And I want that fuckin' suitcase back.' She spoke the last sentence as she closed the door.

Dermot took the boy's suitcase and took the boy's tiny hand in his. Then father and son walked out of The Jarro. When they came to the corner of North Earl Street and

Gardiner Street, Dermot sat down on the snow-covered steps of Moran's Hotel. The boy stood in front of him with his hands deep in his pockets.

'What's your name?' The boy asked.

'Dermot, Dermot Browne, son.'

'You're the man that was standin' outside our school, aren't yeh?'

'You saw me?' Dermot asked.

'Yes. Aunt Margaret said not to mind you. But I will.'

'You will what?'

'I will mind you. You look like you need mindin'.'

Dermot laughed aloud. Without removing his hands from his duffle coat pockets the boy sat down on the steps beside Dermot. For a few minutes the two sat in silence. It was the boy that spoke first. 'What are we goin' to do now?'

'Son – I was just asking meself the same question!'

Chapter 21

AGNES WAS HAPPY BUT WORRIED as she returned the receiver to its cradle. She walked slowly into the kitchen and was about to tell Pierre to put the kettle on, but it was too late, he already had a pot of tea made. When she sat at the kitchen table, Pierre placed her mug and an ashtray in front of her. Agnes was in a slight daze, still trying to get it all straightened out in her head.

'I take it that was Trevor?' Pierre asked.

'Yes. He has the boy!' Agnes answered.

'What boy?'

'Cormac, young Cormac.'

'*Trevor* has Cormac?' Pierre was amazed.

Agnes snapped out of her daze and began to explain the situation to Pierre. 'No, *Dermot* has the boy. He took him from Margaret O'Brien yesterday. He got on the 'phone to Trevor, and said he's coming over with the boy to stay with Trevor for a while.'

'Why?'

'He told Trevor that he had nowhere else to go – sure he could come here, for God's sake,' Agnes exclaimed.

Pierre didn't answer. He knew that Dermot wouldn't be coming here. He also knew that Agnes knew it. So he made no comment. Agnes looked over at the kitchen window. Outside she could see the swirling snow. It was a cold, nasty night.

'Christ, I hope they'll be all right travelling in that weather!'

*   *   *

It was a harrowing journey. The boat trip to Holyhead was wild and uncomfortable. The boat was packed with people returning from their Christmas trip home to the 'old sod'. The train journey to Manchester felt like it was going to go on forever. They changed at Crewe from a chilly train into a freezing train.

On the way Dermot discovered a lot about his new-found son. For instance, he liked to talk. And questions – the kid loved questions. Not just ordinary questions, like how fast does the train go, but questions from left-field. Cormac asked Dermot three questions in succession that had no relation to each other. The first one was: 'Is God in England?' Dermot had little trouble in explaining to Cormac that God was everywhere, wherever you wanted him to be. Next came: 'Why does Aunt Margaret shave under her arms?' Dermot told him it was because she had to shave somewhere, and she didn't have a beard. Dermot went into hysterics when Cormac replied, 'Yes she does!' Also, Cormac was not happy to be pawned off with simple answers. Which made his next question all the more difficult.

'Who made you my Daddy?'

Dermot thought about this for a few moments. He looked out the window of the train into the dark English countryside as if searching for an answer.

'I did!' he finally said.

'How?'

It's always the one-syllable questions that are the most difficult. Dermot held up the index finger of each of his hands and held them about six inches apart. And he began to explain.

'Let's say this finger is a man and he has lots of love to give, and this finger over here is a woman and she has lots of love to give.' Dermot now pushed the two fingers together. 'So they get together and they give each other lots of love. But they soon find that they have too much love to give, so they need somebody to share it with. Along comes a little baby boy, and that boy is you.' Dermot smiled as he said this last bit and poked his two fingers joined together into Cormac's ribs. The boy laughed; it was the first time Dermot had heard the child laugh, ever. He liked the sound of it.

'And did you have lots of love for my mammy?' the boy asked.

Dermot looked into Cormac's eyes. In them he could see Mary Carter, except without the pain.

'Yes ... I did.' Dermot stood up. 'I'm going to the toilet, you stay here and don't move.' Dermot walked the length of the carriage and locked himself in a little triangular-shaped toilet. Looking in the mirror he ran his fingers through his hair. He then sat on the toilet bowl and began to count his money, again. He had four hundred and ten pounds. If he could bum his accommodation off Trevor for just two or three weeks, and in the meantime get himself fixed up with a job, he would have enough to get a flat. After that he decided he would just take it day by day. When he came out of the toilet Dermot went to the buffet counter and bought two cups of Bovril and two bread rolls. He returned to the seat and virtually had to force-feed the boy the Bovril. When Cormac eventually finished his cup there came more questions.

'Do I have to call you Daddy now?'

'You don't have to do anything. Do you *want* to call me Daddy?'

Cormac thought for a moment or two and then said, 'No.'

'All right then.' But Dermot was disappointed. 'Why don't you call me Dermot until we get to know each other better and then if you want to you can call me Daddy, all right?'

'Yes, that's all right.' The boy seemed satisfied.

The questions continued for the next forty-five minutes and Dermot was relieved when they eventually reached Manchester. They alighted from the train and walked down the platform. As the ticket checker was taking the tickets from them, Dermot was glancing around the crowd to see if he could spot Trevor. He very nearly didn't recognise him.

'Dermot! Over here, Dermo,' came a voice from the crowd.

Dermot followed the direction of the voice with his eyes until they fell upon a handsome, robust young man with sandy blond hair, wearing a navy business suit. Dermot's immediate thought was, what has happened to my scrawny little teenage brother? As the distance between the two men shortened, Trevor's face lit up with a smile and Dermot was wrapped in a hug of genuine warmth and welcome, such as he hadn't felt in a long time. He felt safe. The drive from the station to Altringham was one of rushed questions and half-answers, with both men eventually deciding they would wait till they got back to the house, as some of the answers were awkward for Dermot with the boy sitting in the back of the car. One tricky item that arose was when Dermot said to Trevor, 'I don't want you to tell Mammy I'm here. Or that I have the boy. I have to sort this out myself, Trevor.'

Trevor was perplexed and he hoped it didn't show in his answer. 'Mammy? Oh yeh, sure, Dermot. Whatever you say.'

Within forty minutes of leaving the station, Cormac was stripped, washed and tucked up in bed in the spare bedroom of Trevor's home. Within one minute of being tucked up he was asleep. The boy was exhausted. Still, for five more minutes Dermot stood over the bed and stared at him. He tried to push to the back of his mind the enormity of the task he had undertaken: raising a child. He could barely look after himself. Dermot left the bedroom and went downstairs to the brightly-lit kitchen.

Maria was busying herself at the table preparing a place for Dermot and putting some food down on it.

'Oh God, Maria, you shouldn't have bothered cooking anything!' Dermot said half-apologetically.

'Nonsense, it's just a cup of tea and a toasted sandwich. Sit down, Dermot. I've heard so much about you from Trevor. Prison life can't be easy – it must be great to be out and about again.'

Dermot was taken aback by the openness and frankness of the girl. She had managed to convey in one sentence that she knew Dermot had been in prison for a long time and there was no need for him to tiptoe around the subject. He relaxed. He liked her, and he envied Trevor. The three of them sat at the kitchen table and

Trevor opened up the conversation with, 'So, bring me up to speed on what's been happening.'

Between mouthfuls of toasted sandwich, and over four mugs of tea and uncountable cigarettes, Dermot relayed his experiences since he had left Mountjoy. He told them of his row with Mark. He tried to explain what he was trying to achieve in making these first few steps out of prison alone. He touched on the bitterness he felt against his mother, whom Trevor was tempted to defend, but catching a sideways glance from Maria, he let it go. Dermot told them of how he was drawn to the boy, and his realisation that the boy was his son. He even made them laugh when he described his collecting the boy from Margaret O'Brien's. When he had finished, it dawned on Dermot that this was the longest conversation he had had with anyone in nearly seven years.

'So what now, Dermot?' Trevor asked.

'I don't know. Take it a day at a time, I suppose. Got to get a job, and try and get a place of my own, with the kid of course. God, I have to think about getting the kid into a school. But first things first.' Dermot put his hand in his back pocket and withdrew his bundle of money. He peeled off five ten-pound notes and pushed them across the table to Trevor. Maria's eyes lit up.

'There's the fifty quid you sent me, I really appreciated it. Thanks a lot, Trevor.'

'No, no, that was a gift, Dermot, not a loan!' Trevor pushed the money back.

'I'd feel better if you took it, Trevor, I really would.' Dermot pushed the money back to Trevor.

'Don't be ridiculous.' Trevor pushed the money back again.

Maria was following the money like a tennis ball. When Dermot eventually won the argument and Trevor took the money, Maria had it spent before he even got it into his pocket.

'I'll make more tea!' Maria announced, and went to the sink to fill the kettle. The kitchen door creaked as it opened and there, standing in the doorway, wearing only one of Maria's tee-shirts as a nightshirt, and rubbing his eyes, stood young Cormac. He was disorientated and a little frightened.

'What are you doing down?' Dermot asked.

The boy walked to Dermot and Dermot picked him up and sat him on his lap. Maria looked over her shoulder and smiled at the scene. It was nice to have a child in the house. Her smile died when the boy asked Dermot, 'Dermot, where's me mammy?'

Dermot became uncomfortable. He looked from Trevor to Maria and then back at the boy. The boy's pale face was turned towards Dermot's. He expected an answer.

'Your mammy died, Cormac,' Dermot answered, averting his eyes from the boy's gaze.

'What's *died*, Dermot?' the boy asked.

How do you explain 'died' to a child? Dermot thought. The quiet in the kitchen was broken by the clicking sound of Maria turning on the kettle. She leaned her back against the kitchen sink and crossed her arms as Dermot sat the boy up on the table facing him.

'Died is like changing from what you are into something better, more beautiful.' The boy's face was puzzled. 'Once upon a time,' Dermot began, 'there was a pond. And in this pond there lived many, many different things.

138

Things like frogs, little fish, spiders, and right at the bottom of the pond lived lots and lots of grubs. Growing right out of the middle of the pond, from the bottom right through the water out into the sunny air, was a long blade of grass.'

Dermot could see he had the boy's interest. So he went on: 'Every now and then one of the grubs would climb up the blade of grass, right up to the top and out of the water, and would never be seen again! So, one day all the grubs got together and decided that one of them should go up the blade of grass, out of the water, see what was there, and come back and tell the rest of them, so that they would know.

'One of the little grubs stepped forward and said that he would go. And all the other grubs clapped at his bravery. He set off on his journey, crawling up the blade of grass. He was so tiny that he didn't even move the grass as he climbed along it. Halfway up, he looked down to see all his little friends staring up at him, eagerly waiting. He climbed some more. Just as he came to where the grass left the water, he turned to look at his friends one more time. They were waving and smiling and he waved back.

'Then, taking a big breath, he climbed up the blade of grass out of the water. At first he felt no different, so he climbed on until he got right to the top of the blade of grass. Then, in the blazing sunshine, a wondrous thing happened. The little grub changed into a magnificent dragonfly. He was green and yellow and blue, and had four wings. At first he didn't know what the wings were for, but when he flapped them he took off and began to fly. He flew around the pond, and frogs would look up and say, "Look at that beautiful dragonfly."

'But now he couldn't get back into the pond to tell his friends. Still, he knew they would find out for themselves some day. So, flapping his wings he took off into the warm sunshine with a great big smile on his face.

'So you see, Cormac, that's what "died" is. Your mammy has become a dragonfly!'

When the story ended Cormac smiled. 'Oh goodie!' he exclaimed as he threw his arms around Dermot's neck.

'Now, son, it's bed for you!' and Dermot carried the boy back upstairs. Within minutes the boy was asleep again and Dermot returned to the kitchen. When he sat down he sensed the riveted attention of both Trevor and Maria. He looked from one to the other, eventually holding his arms in the air and asking, 'What? What's wrong?'

'Where did you hear that story, Dermot?' Trevor asked.

'I just made it up. Why?'

Trevor didn't answer. Instead he turned to Maria and said, 'Maria, this is it – the real thing!' But Maria was already on her way to the writing desk to get some paper. They asked Dermot to write the story out exactly as he had told it to young Cormac. An air of excitement filled the kitchen.

Chapter 22

IT WAS AT PIERRE'S SIXTIETH BIRTHDAY PARTY in Wolfe Tone
Grove that Betty announced she was expecting her
second child. Agnes was thrilled at the thought of a fifth
grandchild. The gathering in the kitchen included Agnes,
her sons Mark, Rory and Simon, her daughters-in-law
Fiona and Betty, and her friend Carmel Dowdall, and the
kitchen was now abuzz with 'baby talk'. The boys were
feeling uncomfortable enough on the edges of this conversation, but when Betty exclaimed that she hoped her
next birth wouldn't take as long as her last, and then
Agnes burst in with 'Don't talk to me about long deliveries.
I was so long in labour on me fourth that they had to
shave me twice!' the boys made a hurried exit, while the
girls howled with laughter.

The boys joined the rest of the party in the sitting room.
In there, Pierre and Mr Brady, Buster's father and Agnes's
next-door neighbour – a baker – were discussing the
different techniques of baking. Mr Brady was passing on
tips to Pierre that could be useful in Pierre's pizza
business. Pierre, on the other hand, while recognising the
convenience of the sliced pan, was explaining to Mr Brady
that only in France could 'real' bread be bought.

Pierre noticed that Rory seemed to be wandering aimlessly through the party, so he excused himself and went to join Agnes's third-eldest son.

'Dino is not coming then, Rory?' Pierre got straight to the point.

'No, Pierre.' Rory looked down into his glass and added, 'It's over, Pierre, he's gone!'

'Don't be silly, Rory, you two have fought before. You will see, in a few days everything will be all right.'

Rory shook his head. 'No, Pierre, this time it's over for real. I blame that fuckin' shop, we should never have opened it!'

'The shop' that Rory was referring to was a hairdressing salon in Prussia Street named The Lazy Curl. Rory and Dino had indeed at last made the move to go into business for themselves. The premises had been a salon before, but not a very successful one, so the two men took a lease on the building in the hopes that they could turn it around. They didn't. Where it's not always true that lovers do not make good business partners, unfortunately in the case of Rory and Dino it was. The real problem was that, although both of them were excellent stylists, when it came to business neither of them knew their arse from their elbow. Also, jealousy began to creep in. The salon was unisex, and any man that came in to get his hair done by Rory would find himself attended to by Dino also, who would be sweeping up imaginary hairs from under the man's feet, at the same time poking in little comments at Rory like, 'God, that man's hair must be very difficult, it's taking you so long.'

Or if Rory was engaging a man in friendly conversation Dino would pop by and say, 'Ah, Rory, it's great to hear you laughing; you go on ahead, don't mind me. I'm just going to unblock the toilet.' After which the toilet door would slam.

While Rory tried to convince Dino that what he was doing was called PR, and was essential for business, Dino insisted that what Rory was doing was called flirting. Eventually the bills outweighed the profits. The shop closed after only ten months, although both men went straight into good positions in other salons.

This was the first time in ten years that the two men had been parted during working hours, and the parting began to put a strain on their relationship. They had one or two rows, after which one or the other would leave, but then return the next day, and the making up would nearly make the row worthwhile. But this last row was serious. Rory knew it was the end when Dino began dividing up the CDs, most especially when Dino insisted on keeping all the Leonard Cohen ones for himself. In a deep depression, Dino moved out into an apartment in Rathgar, and Rory returned to his mother's.

When Rory had recounted the latter part of this story to Pierre, Pierre's face was very serious. 'He took the Leonard Cohens? Mmm, that *is* serious, Rory!'

They both smartened up when they were joined by Agnes. 'How yis? Great night, isn't it?' she said brightly.

'Yes,' the two men answered, virtually in harmony.

'And Betty pregnant. Did you hear the whinin' out of her? Jesus, at her age I was on me seventh!'

'Ah, Mammy, couples today aren't like that, they don't have as many children,' Rory exclaimed.

'Yes, that's true, Rory, and they don't have as much fun in bed either!' Now Pierre winked at Agnes and the two of them began to giggle like teenagers.

'Ah, here, you two are making me sick,' was Rory's parting shot as he went to mingle.

'He seems a bit down,' Agnes commented to Pierre when Rory was out of earshot.

'Yes, he is a little. Oh, I'm sure everything will sort itself out. So, you are enjoying yourself, Agnes?'

'Of course I am. Jesus, Pierre, sixty! Where did the time go?' Agnes mused. 'It's a pity Cathy didn't make it tonight. Still, I'll have her home in the morning!'

As the party was in full swing in Finglas, Cathy O'Leary and her boyfriend were loading her luggage and the baby's things into a car in Arklow. Her intention was to move herself and Pamela in with her mother for a few months until she got herself sorted. Mark had promised her a job in Senga Furnishings, and Agnes had agreed to take Pamela during Cathy's working hours. Once settled, Cathy intended to get herself a place of her own, or co-habit with her boyfriend; she hadn't decided yet. One thing she had decided was that Mick O'Leary was about to become a bachelor again. The breaking of the news to Mick had been one of the shortest conversations Cathy and Mick had ever had.

'I'm moving back in with me mother, and I'm taking Pamela with me,' Cathy had declared.

Her husband was sitting on an armchair with his feet on a footstool. He had a newspaper on his lap and the television was switched on with the sound turned down. Mick's eyes were fixed on the screen as he watched a boxing match. He seemed to enter into the match himself, going with every punch, his muscles tightening at each throw. Mick did not respond; he didn't even turn his head. Cathy awaited some kind of reply.

'I couldn't give a shite,' Mick eventually said, telling his wife the truth for the first time in many years.

Cathy sat in the front passenger seat of the car, with Pamela sleeping on her lap, as they sped through the night towards Dublin city. Between the towns of Rathnew and Bray, Cathy had a silent cry. Her boyfriend-and-driver looked straight ahead, not wishing to intrude on the beginning of the woman's healing.

Chapter 23

WHEN YOU CONSIDER THE EVENTUAL SUCCESS over the next few years of Dermot Browne's stories, it's hard to believe how close *Dragonfly* came to not happening. Within six weeks of Dermot recounting the story, thanks to the hard work of both Maria and Trevor on the illustrations, *Dragonfly* was ready to go to print. Unfortunately, the printer decided he wanted to be paid up to date before he would print any further books for Nicholson Books. There followed twenty-four hours of depression, which was lifted when miraculously Geoffrey Collington, the printer, called to say that he would do this one last book on credit, but no more! Trevor was delighted, but wondered what it was that had changed the printer's mind.

Maria Browne knew exactly what it was. Vescoli and White Advertising Agency channelled at least thirty thousand pounds worth of business a year through Collington Printers. Tony Vescoli called Geoffrey Collington and agreed to personally guarantee payment of any outstanding Nicholson Books debts in three months if Collington's would go ahead and print *Dragonfly*. That was when Mr Collington had his miraculous change of heart. Maria would not tell Trevor about this. Her husband was a proud man. Tony's guarantee was never called upon.

Sales of *Dragonfly* were healthy enough right from the start, but when Peter Ustinov chose it as his subject for reading on BBC's *Jackanory* storytime, the sales went through the roof! Dermot Browne received a generous royalty on sales of *Dragonfly*, and, anxious to hang on to their talented brother and have him involved in the business, Trevor and Maria also offered Dermot a fifteen-percent shareholding in the company if he agreed to come up with four more stories. This Dermot did. His latest offering was a story about two young boys whose parents were treating them so badly that they ran away from home. For research Dermot called upon his memory of the many days spent with Buster by the river in Finglas. The book was of course named *Chestnut Hole*. It was a huge hit with young readers and it gained Dermot the Young People's Writer of the Year Award in 1991. In the time between the telling of a tale in his brother's kitchen to the award, just three years had passed, and Dermot Browne had established himself as one of the most prominent children's fiction writers in the United Kingdom.

Nicholson Books now had thirty-one titles on the shelves of bookshops throughout the United Kingdom and Ireland. Along with Dermot Browne, they had also attracted Wilbur Livingston to their increasingly talented stable. Needless to say, Trevor and Maria were delighted with the success of the company, but not complacent. They were careful to consolidate each step forward before risking another new writer, with the result that the company's growth was very solid. Their best year yet came in 1991. Dermot's fifteen-percent shareholding was in good hands. But what really set them all up was three film deals that were made for Dermot's titles. Two major feature films were already in production, and a third was in preparation. Dermot had struck gold.

While Trevor and Maria had now taken up an option to buy the house they had previously been renting and make it their permanent home, Dermot still rented his home. Trevor urged him to buy a place of his own, but Dermot insisted he was happy to carry on renting. In the back of his mind, like all Irish exiles, Dermot still harboured thoughts of moving back to live in Dublin. He could write just as easily from there. Cormac, now ten years old and growing fast, looked more like his father the older he got. He was doing well at school. He was a bright kid and nobody was surprised when he took the district under-eleven public speaking championship award.

Dermot lived very comfortably. He was happy to take his money in dribs and drabs as it came from Nicholson Books, and on only one occasion asked Trevor for a substantial loan. It was for two thousand pounds, which he told Trevor he was sending home to Buster Brady.

Buster, it seemed, had decided to start up his own little gardening business and Dermot was borrowing the money from Trevor to loan it to Buster. Trevor called it an advance rather than a loan and deducted it from future royalty payments. Buster, Dermot told Trevor later, paid back the loan within eighteen months. The business was going well for Buster.

Trevor was pleased to see Dermot settled and enjoying his parenthood of Cormac so much. Life at last, he felt, had taken a turn for the better for his older brother. The only sad part for Trevor was that, despite his encouragement, Dermot had still not spoken to his mother, and Trevor knew how much this was hurting both of them. Maria had assured her husband that given time these things would sort themselves out and she urged him not to interfere. Trevor followed Maria's advice though it broke his heart to do so.

Chapter 24

IT IS SAID THAT THERE IS A CHILD IN US ALL. Or is it maybe that for brief periods in our time as adults we return to our childhood? For instance, is it the child in us that plans surprise parties? Is it the child in us that makes us feel so excited as we hand out our Christmas presents to friends and family? Whatever it is, it was a childlike excitement that filled Dermot Browne's heart as he planned the surprise he had in store for Buster Brady. It all began one morning when Buster's letter arrived on Dermot's mat at his home in Manchester.

Flat 2c
The Villas
Cabra
Dublin 7

16th February 1992

Dear Dermo,

I am in receipt of yours of the 27th inst. The business is going well. With spring just around the corner I expect to be busier than ever, I have seven large gardens now which I am tending on a contract basis and the few bob is coming in. You wont believe it but one of the contracts I have started recently is the grounds around Finglas Garda Station. Its gas how times change things isnt it?

I have just finished reading 'Chestnut Hole', its brilliant! I can recognise so many of the places and stories in it, it was like a trip down memory lane. You know Dermot, those nights we spent sleeping over in Chestnut Hole when you would tell me stories till I fell asleep were great times, I wouldnt change them for a million pounds.

Speaking of loads of money, this brings me to my next news. There is a house for sale in Kilbride (see newspaper clipping enclosed). Its a big house with five bedrooms, on about six acres. Dont panic, Im not thinking of buying the big house, the gardening business isnt that good. But on the edge of the grounds there is a gate keepers lodge. Its not huge but it has two bedrooms and has been recently done up. So I have been on to the auctioneer to see if it was possible to buy the gate lodge separate from the big house. He says he doesnt think its a possibility with the current owner, but believes that a new owner might be attracted to the idea as it will take some of the financial pressure off the cost of the house. Well wait and see, Ill write to you as soon as I have any more news.

Your brother Mark has been a great help, four of the customers that I have were introduced to me by him. He has also helped to keep my books and God knows I need help with them. I would rather do ten gardens than do one set of books.

I hope this letter finds you as it left me, fit and well.

Your friend always,
Buster Brady.

Dermot read the newspaper cutting with interest. He immediately rang the auctioneers in Dublin to get more details on the house. He didn't even know where Kilbride was. The information he received from the auctioneer was quite pleasing. Kilbride was midway between Finglas and Ratoath. It was a nice area and had a good school nearby. The asking price for the main house, the five and three-quarter acres of land, and the gate lodge was £132,000. The house had been built in 1896. Little was done to the house over the next eighty-four years until a German gentleman, a Mr Helmut Schtoll, had purchased the premises in 1980. He had completely gutted both the main building and the gate lodge and refurbished them over the following two years. Herr Schtoll enjoyed the experience so much that he had now decided to buy another property, this time in the west of Ireland, and repeat the procedure. Thus the Kilbride house was up for sale.

Dermot immediately wrote off to the auctioneers making them an offer of £128,000. The auctioneers' reply when it came contained a revised asking price of £130,000 which Dermot had expected. This time in his reply the auctioneer went on to mention a Mr Brady. Mr Brady, the auctioneer explained, was a bachelor, and a gardener by trade. The auctioneer suggested that Mr Brady was 'keen' on purchasing the gate lodge only and that Dermot might consider an offer from Mr Brady of around £28,000. This, the auctioneer explained, meant that Mr Browne would then be paying only £102,000 for the big house and the grounds. Dermot's next move was to accept the new asking price. However, in his reply he also suggested to the auctioneer that he approach Mr Brady with the following proposition: that Mr Brady was being offered by the new owner a lease of ninety-nine years on the gate lodge premises. For this lease Mr Browne would be seeking one hundred pounds per month plus the services of Mr Brady as the groundsman for the five and three-quarter acres that surrounded the big house. Dermot also insisted that in his dealings with Mr Brady the auctioneer should refer to Mr Browne only as 'the client'. Any introductions beyond that, Dermot said, he would take care of when he took possession of the house.

The offer was accepted, although the auctioneer suggested to Dermot that there were other very fine gardeners in that area that would be only too glad to pay a little more than Mr Brady was being asked to pay for the use of the gate lodge. In Dermot's last letter to the auctioneer he thanked him for his services and his advice, but said that he was happy to be doing business with Mr Brady. From then on the deal was left in the hands of solicitors and Dermot eagerly awaited Buster's next letter. It came within two days of the deal being finalised.

Flat 2c
The Villas
Cabra
Dublin 7

25th April 1992

Dear Dermo,

Great news. Do you remember that gate lodge I was telling you about that I was chasing? Well I got it! And listen to this! The deal I got was a ninety-nine year lease on the gate lodge and all I have to pay is one hundred pounds a month, and do the gardens for the new owner. It was a tough deal, many hours of negotiating with the new owner, he was a tough nut to crack. But I stuck to me guns and came out on top. Great isnt it!

I move into the gate lodge in a weeks time, and the new owner moves in another two weeks after that. The gate lodge has two bedrooms so when you come over on a trip with Cormac youll be able to stay with me. I am so excited, every time I think about it I nearly piss in me pants. Ha Ha! So after next week my new address will be 'Chestnut Hole', The Lodge, Manor House, Kilbride, Co. Dublin.

Do you like the name? I got a name plate made down the garden centre and the first thing Ill be doing when I move in is to screw it up on the door. Ill send you some photographs as soon as I move in.

Dermot, I have lots of other stuff to tell you, but Id rather wait till you come home and visit so we could be face to face when were talking, do you know what I mean? Until then;

I hope this letter finds you as it leaves me, fit and well.

Your friend always,
Buster Brady.
(Gardener and Property Owner)

Dermot laughed until he cried when he read the bit about the 'tough negotiations'. It just made the surprise he was about to spring on Buster all the sweeter.

By the end of that week Dermot's furniture, Cormac's toys, and most of their clothes were boxed, packed into a removals van and shipped off to the new house in Kilbride in Ireland. For the last week, while he tidied up the remainder of his business affairs, Dermot had moved out of his rented accommodation and in with Trevor and Maria. On the Wednesday of that week, Maria and Trevor threw a huge house party so that all of those people who had come to know Dermot would have an opportunity to say goodbye.

Dermot and Trevor looked remarkably alike. But as the two men circulated, one of their differences became very obvious. While Dermot was telling all of the guests how excited he was about going home to Ireland and how beautiful the new house was, and describing in detail the wondrous gardens that surrounded it, Trevor, on the other hand, was explaining to everybody the tax advantages of living on an island whose government regards its writers and artists as national treasures and treats them accordingly. Still, a great night was had by all and when all of the guests were gone and Cormac and Maria were at last asleep, the two brothers poured themselves a drink. In the bright kitchen of the now-silent house, Trevor lifted his glass and said, 'To Mrs Browne's Boys, God bless them all.'

For a couple of moments Dermot looked into Trevor's face. When he was satisfied that this was not a cynical jab at him by Trevor, but a genuine celebration of the ups and downs of their family, Dermot smiled and the glasses went clink.

To leave your country as an ex-convict as Dermot had, and then to return as a successful writer, or indeed a success in any field, as Dermot was now doing, is a source of great satisfaction. Unless the capital city of that country happens to be Dublin. Beautiful Dublin city, with its ancient buildings and artistic heritage, just entering its second millennium, has a way of bringing you right back down to earth. Dermot drove off the ferry at the North Wall Quay and when he reached the security barrier at the exit, the security man did a double-take on him:

'You're, eh, Dermot Browne, aren't you?' Chuffed with the thought that his success as a writer had reached the man-in-the-street in Dublin, Dermot looked to his son full of pride and then back to the security man and answered, 'Yes, actually, I am!' and smiled.

The smile soon faded as the man replied, 'I knew I recognised you, you're one of Agnes Browne's twins, aren't you?'

Dermot drove away without reply. At the Brian Ború pub in Phibsboro, Dermot and Cormac stopped for a coffee and a sandwich. Here Dermot was recognised yet again, but this time as Mark Browne's brother. And even on the drive out towards Kilbride, just beyond Finglas, when Dermot was stopped at a police road block, the Garda recognised Dermot as Buster Brady's friend.

'Welcome home, Dermot,' Dermot muttered to himself as he drove away from the road block. In the village of Kilbride he wasn't recognised at all, either as anybody's brother, son or friend, or even as a writer. There, from some of the friendly locals, he received directions to his new home. Naturally, each offer of directions was preceeded with a little conversation, and it was mid-morning by the time they came to the gates of the house in Kilbride. Dermot drove across the cattle grid at the gates and stopped just beyond the gate lodge. There was smoke coming from the lodge chimney. Obviously somebody was home. Dermot was surprised to see a young child playing in the back garden of the gate lodge. He wondered if maybe the old tenants had not moved out yet, or whether Buster's plans to move had been delayed. He decided to settle into his own house before finding out what the story was and he drove on up to the magnificent building.

In one of the letters Dermot had received from the auctioneer, the agent had described the part-time housekeeper who had been working at the house for some five years, a Mrs Annette Dolan, as a hard-working woman. The agent suggested Dermot might consider keeping her on. Accompanying this letter was a recommendation from Herr Schtoll, listing the virtues of Mrs Dolan, and ending in a suggestion identical to that of the agent. Dermot knew he would need help in the house anyway, so he decided that, certainly for the time being, Mrs Dolan should indeed remain in the house. It was a wise decision. No sooner were he and Cormac out of the car than the front door was opened by a plump, jolly-looking woman in a snow-white apron.

'Hello, hello and welcome,' the woman declared, with her arms wide open, and she tripped down the steps like a ballet dancer. She was very nimble for her age, which Dermot guessed to be about fifty-five.

'Well, now, you must be Cormac! I've been looking forward to meeting you,' she said, and with a beaming smile extended her hand. Cormac returned the smile and shook hands very formally with the woman. She then turned to Dermot.

'*Céad míle fáilte*, Mr Browne, and if you don't mind me saying so, I can see where young Cormac gets his looks.' The woman reddened a little and rocked with laughter.

Cormac giggled. Dermot could tell Mrs Dolan was going to be with them for a long time to come.

'*Go raibh maith agat*, Mrs Dolan, and it is indeed a pleasure to meet you too. Herr Schtoll recommended you very highly and already I can see why.'

The woman brushed down her apron and fixed her hair, at the same time saying, 'Why, thank you, Mr Browne. I can see with that charm of yours I'm going to have to watch myself around here.' Then she roared laughing again, and this time Cormac didn't confine himself to a giggle but laughed aloud.

Within an hour the car had been emptied of luggage and Dermot and Cormac, hand-in-hand, had examined every inch of the house. Cormac then ate a bowl of cereal and tore off into the fields to explore this new land of adventure. Dermot was standing at the large kitchen window looking down at the gate lodge and sipping a cup of hot tea while behind him at the solid fuel stove Mrs Dolan was cooking up a fry. The sizzle of the rashers and the beautiful smell of frying sausages was so familiar that it sent thoughts of his mother flitting through Dermot's mind. He lit himself a cigarette and went back to watching the gate lodge. Once again he caught sight of the sandy-haired little girl bobbing across the small back garden of the gate lodge.

'Mrs Dolan, whose child is that?'

Mrs Dolan hurried to the kitchen window, wiping her hands in a tea towel as she walked. 'Which child would that be now, Mr Browne?'

'That child, down there,' Dermot said, pointing at the gate lodge.

'Oh now, that would be Mr Brady's child!'

'Mr Brady's child?' Dermot's question came out with a surprised tone.

'Well, now, I'm not one for gossip, but –' Mrs Dolan began with the gossip's usual opening line, '– there's a couple of local men in the village have had a pint with Mr Brady and the word is that it's the child of his girlfriend. They're not married.' Mrs Dolan whispered this last part and looked as if she were going to bless herself as soon as she said it. Dermot couldn't believe it. Buster with a girlfriend and a child? Why hadn't he mentioned any of this in his letters? Just then Dermot saw a battered Ford Escort pull up at the gate lodge and out stepped Buster Brady. He was a lot trimmer than Dermot remembered him.

'That's Mr Brady now,' exclaimed Mrs Dolan, and both she and Dermot took in the scene as the young child ran from the back garden into Buster's arms. Mrs Dolan smiled, Dermot frowned. When Mrs Dolan's sideways glance caught sight of Dermot's frown she misinterpreted his look. 'He's not lazy at all, you know, oh no, I put him to work the very first day he moved in. Sure he's done all those flower beds over on that side, look.' Mrs Dolan pointed to the west side of the garden. Dermot's gaze didn't leave Buster and the child.

'So you've met him then?' Dermot asked.

'Indeed I did. He was only in the door and he came up here to introduce himself. A nice man! Rough as a bear's arse, but a nice man.'

'You didn't mention who the new owner of the house was, did you?'

'Absolutely not! Herr Schtoll was adamant about that. He told me that you insisted on doing the introductions yourself, so I said nothing. Not a word.' As she said this Mrs Dolan pulled an imaginary zip across her lips.

'Good,' Dermot answered. He turned back to the window while Mrs Dolan went back to the preparation of food. 'How many rashers would you like, Mr Browne?' she asked.

'Better put on plenty, we're about to have a visitor,' Dermot answered. Buster was walking up the drive with the child in hand. Dermot stood back from the window, but followed Buster's every step.

* * *

It was when Buster had pulled into the hardware store in Kilbride village to pick up some chicken-wire that Elsie McGrath, the wife of the store's owner, was eager to tell him the news.

'Your man has arrived,' she announced, as if she were announcing the results of an election.

'What?' Buster was puzzled.

'Your man – the new fella from the big house. He has arrived.'

'He's here? You're kiddin'. I thought he wasn't comin' till tomorrow.'

'Well, he's here today. Probably trying to catch you on the hop, Mr Brady.'

Buster collected his goods, loaded them into the car and headed for home. Within minutes he pulled up outside 'Chestnut Hole'. As he was climbing out of his car he got his first clue about the new owner. Parked right outside the big house was a shiny white Rover 3000. It had yellow number plates. English ones. Buster's attention was diverted by the call of his name.

'Buster! Buster, you're home!' the little girl called as she ran into his arms.

'Yes love, I'm home,' Buster chuckled as he scooped the little girl up.

'Mammy is making dinner, are you coming in?'

'We'll go in now in a minute.' He put the child down. 'But first why don't you and me go up and introduce ourselves to the new man?' He took the little girl by the hand and they began to stroll up the driveway.

'Is he a nice man, Buster?' The child asked.

'I don't know, love, I hope so. I also hope he notices the bit of work I done on those flower beds!' As they approached the house Buster was looking at every window, searching for any sign of life. There was none. When they reached the top of the gravel driveway, instead of going immediately to the front door Buster began to examine the car. He peered in through the windows for any tell-tale signs of what this man might be like. On the floor behind the driver's seat was a half-full bottle of Coca-Cola and some sweet papers. On the front passenger seat was a pair of sunglasses. No help at all.

'It's a big car, Buster,' the little girl remarked.

'Yes, love, it certainly is. Right, let's knock at the door and see who we meet.'

*   *   *

Dermot watched as Buster circled the car. He had lost weight. It suited him. He saw Buster look up at the house one more time and then disappear from view as he walked into the porch. The doorbell sounded.

'I'll get that, Mr Browne.' Mrs Dolan began to wipe her hands yet again in the towel.

'No, that's all right, Mrs Dolan, you carry on with breakfast, I'll get it meself.' As Dermot walked to the door, he stopped and felt his chin. He hadn't shaved. It wouldn't be the first time Buster had seen him unshaven, he thought, smiling. He took a deep breath, turned the latch and opened the door wide. The sound of Buster Brady's jawbone was nearly audible as his chin dropped. The two men stood in silence for a couple of seconds, but it seemed like an hour.

Dermot broke the deadlock. 'So, you must be Mr Brady?'

With just one leap from Buster the two men were wrapped in each other's arms. Mrs Dolan heard the commotion and emerged from the kitchen to see the two men embracing and crying.

'I certainly hope you don't intend to treat all the staff like this, Mr Browne,' she exclaimed. The two men burst into laughter. The embrace stopped, although Dermot still held an arm around Buster's shoulder.

'Mrs Dolan, let me introduce you to Mr Buster Brady. This man, Mrs Dolan, has been my friend, and sometimes my only friend,' he looked at Buster, 'for as long as I can remember.' The men smiled at each other.

'You bastard!' Buster cried as they hugged once again.

Now Cormac had arrived back to the house and was standing on the doorstep. The little girl stood at a distance, watching quietly. Cormac took in the scene. Dermot introduced him to Buster.

Buster got down on one knee and opened his arms wide for the boy, who was approaching with his hand outstretched for a handshake. 'I knew you, Cormac, when you were only an egg.' He laughed that warm Buster Brady laugh. The boy smiled and gave him a full embrace.

'Cormac, son,' said Dermot, 'you take the little girl off for a walk, I'll meet her later. Her Daddy and me have a little catching up to do. Come on into the kitchen, Buster!' Dermot put his arm around Buster again and the two men walked into the kitchen like little boys. In recounting the story of the buying of the house and the setting up of the surprise for Buster, which was interrupted with slaps on the back and howls of laughter, an hour soon passed. The doorbell sounded again.

'That's probably the kids back, Mrs Dolan, would you let them in?' Dermot instructed.

'I will indeed, Mr Browne,' Mrs Dolan left the kitchen.

'Jesus, Dermot, isn't all this like a dream come true?' Buster said.

'Dreams *do* come true, Buster, if you work hard enough at them.'

'Your mother used to always say that!' Buster smiled, and then his smile vanished as he realised what he'd said. There was silence for a moment between the two men.

'You two haven't made up then?' Buster asked.

'No, Buster, and it's got more difficult as the years moved on. You know sometimes I can't even remember why we fell out? I think it was because I know she thinks of me as being like me Da, and I learned from a very early age that she hated me Da. Her thinking of me like that really hurt me then. It still hurts me.'

'But that's ridiculous, Dermot. I've talked to her loads of times. She thinks the world of you. She's so proud of you, you know.'

Dermot slapped Buster gently on the shoulder and said, 'Let's not talk about it, Buster, okay?'

'Okay.' Again for a couple of moments there was silence.

Then Dermot smiled that impish smile of his. 'I really caught you, didn't I?' Dermot teased.

'You bastard!' The two men laughed.

'I'll get you back,' Buster promised, and with that Mrs Dolan entered the kitchen.

'Mr Brady – I think you're in trouble! Your wi– Mrs Bra– em, your *woman* is here at the door. Apparently your dinner's been ready for an hour.'

Buster looked at Dermot. 'I just might get you back sooner than you think, Dermot. Mrs Dolan would you show my *woman* in please?'

'I will of course, Mr Brady, if that's all right with you, Mr Browne.'

'Of course it is. Bring the girl in.'

When Mrs Dolan left the kitchen Dermot stood and began to brush the crumbs off his lap, preparing himself to meet Buster's *woman.*

'Did you hear that auld wan, me fuckin' woman – she didn't know what to call her,' Buster remarked. The two men laughed.

Just then the two women entered the room. Dermot's laughter stopped and he stood agape. So did Buster's *woman*!

'Cathy?'

'Dermot? Dermot Browne?'

They rushed at each other and the embrace was a replica of the two men's embrace at the front door an hour earlier.

Mrs Dolan looked at Buster Brady questioningly. 'Now what's the story?' she asked.

Buster smiled and said simply, 'It's his sister.'

'Good God – I have to have a drink.' With that Mrs Dolan vanished into the sitting room.

*   *   *

It had been a good day in Moore Street market. Agnes Browne had virtually sold out, except for a couple of cases of tomatoes and a box of oranges which she would store. They would sell the next day. With her two trestles folded, her canvas hood dismantled and the lot packed onto her trolley, she made her way towards her storage shed. On the way she had to pass the fish stand of Winnie the Mackerel. Winnie was wiping down her marble slab and preparing to close for the evening.

'Good day, Winnie, wasn't it?'

'Great, Agnes. I only have the one salmon left. If I got rid of that it would be a perfect day!'

'Fancy a drink, love?' Agnes asked.

'Be Jaysus I do, Agnes, where? Madigans?'

'Yeh, Madigans!'

The after-work rendezvous confirmed, Agnes headed down the little lane to her storage shed. When she had her stuff packed away and the door locked up for the night she went back up the lane expecting to find Winnie ready to go for the drink. Instead, she found her negotiating with a customer. Agnes listened in to see if Winnie was about to have her perfect day. The woman was well-spoken and obviously from the southside of the city.

'Tell me, dear, am I too late for salmon?'

'Not at all, love!' Winnie rolled up her sleeves and delved with her two arms into the huge bucket of iced

164

water that she had under her stall. She withdrew the salmon and plonked it on the slab.

'This salmon has your name written all over it, missus, would you like me to bone it for you?'

'It's a tiny bit small, do you have a bigger one?'

Winnie dropped the salmon back into the bucket, and looked over her shoulder at Agnes. She gave Agnes a wink.

'Let me have a look, love,' announced Winnie as she delved back into the bucket again. She drew out the same salmon, only this time she plonked it on the slab the opposite way round.

'This one's a bit bigger,' Winnie announced.

'Ah yes, now that's a lovely salmon!' the woman declared.

Winnie again looked over her shoulder and winked at Agnes, but while she was in mid-wink the woman went on, 'I'll take both of them!'

Agnes laughed and wondered what Winnie was going to do to get herself out of this one. Slowly Winnie turned back to the woman. The woman waited expectantly.

'Ah ... I'm sorry, love, I couldn't sell you both of them. You see, I'm having a dinner party meself tonight and I'm goin' to hang on to one of the salmon. So you can either have this one or the smaller one, or none at all.'

'Oh, you're having a dinner party? So am I. I was going to do Salmon Béarnaise, what were you going to do?'

'What? Em ... sandwiches, love. Salmon sandwiches. Now, do you want it or not?'

'Oh well, go on then, I'll take it. That one – the bigger one – I don't want the small one.'

Winnie wrapped the fish and took the money from the woman, dropping it into her purse to complete her perfect day. She tipped over her bucket of iced water into the gutter, loaded her trolley and headed down the lane to store her own stuff.

Agnes roared after her, 'I'll meet you in Madigan's, Winnie,' and headed off to the pub.

*   *   *

Dermot Browne turned his back and pretended to be looking at something in the shop window as Agnes walked past. She didn't notice him. He looked after her as she waddled up Parnell Street. He didn't know what to do next. He'd been hanging around Moore Street for the last hour and a half. He had seen his mother from every angle possible. God, how she had aged. There was more grey than black in her hair now. Her face was a mass of wrinkles and although they gave her face character, they took from the beauty that Dermot had remembered of his mother. He didn't want to approach her in Moore Street with all the other stall holders around; she would have made too big a fuss and he also feared rejection. But he felt better now that he had seen her. As he took his first few steps to walk after her she disappeared in the doorway of Madigan's pub. When he reached the doorway of the pub he stood outside for a few moments, shuffling his feet, trying to decide what to do next. He entered the pub. He looked around casually but he couldn't see her anywhere. Then from behind the frosted glass in the window of the snug he heard her call to the barman.

'A Malibu and pineapple, Arthur, and a pint of cider.'

'Be with you in a minute, Agnes,' the barman called.

Dermot took a high stool right beside the frosted glass panel. When Agnes's drinks were put on the bar they were no more than two feet from where he sat. His mother's wrinkled hands came into view, and he watched the hands busily picking through the coins to extract the price of the drink. The nicotine-stained fingers and the grime from the vegetables thick under her nails were so familiar to Dermot, it reminded him of being a young boy again. He wanted to just reach over and squeeze her hand, but as soon as the money was laid on the bar the hands and the drinks vanished.

The barman turned to Dermot. 'Can I help you, son?'

'Yes, a pint of Guinness,' Dermot said very softly.

The barman went away to begin the slow process of pulling the perfect pint. The pint arrived just as Winnie the Mackerel made her way into the snug. Dermot could hear the conversation clearly.

'Ah, you're a sweetheart, Agnes. What about your woman and the salmon?' The two women laughed. For a few moments there was just the sound of the two glasses being replaced on the table and the swish of a match being struck against a matchbox. Dermot went to the gents' toilet. On the way he called the barman and asked him to put up another round of drinks for the two women in the snug.

The barman glanced down and said, 'I'm just after giving them a round, will I hold on till they're ready for them?'

'Yes, do that.' Dermot gave the man a five-pound note and told him to keep the change. The barman saluted him. Tips were thin on the ground in Parnell Street.

Dermot found himself alone in the toilets. When he had finished at the urinal he washed his hands. As he was drying them under the hot air machine he looked at himself in the mirror. He looked like a scared little boy. He began to talk to his reflection.

'For Christ's sake, if you are ready to end this then so is she. Now just go out there and say: Hello, Mammy. After that just take it as it comes. Now, come on, do it now!' He put his hands one on each side of the sink and hung his head.

'Any news from your Dermot?' Winnie the Mackerel asked as she shook the matchstick to extinguish the flame.

'Not a word, the little bastard!'

'He's home two weeks now, Agnes. I was sure you would have heard from him.'

'So was I. Do you know, Winnie, on the morning he was arriving I had the house spick and span and had the makings of a fry ready. I got up at seven o'clock, lit the fire and laid the table for breakfast for him and the boy. I was sure he would come by on his way to Kilbride. But no, not a word. The little bastard! Pierre slagged me. Told me I shouldn't be getting me hopes up, but I was sure he'd call, if only to let me see Cormac.'

Agnes finished speaking. She took a drag from her cigarette. As she exhaled the smoke she could see through the frosted glass the figure of a man leaning against it as he took his seat on the high stool. She watched as the man's arm reached for a pint of Guinness. On one of the fingers was a single-stone diamond signet ring. That, along with the expensive-looking watch, told her that this man wasn't a local – probably a tourist. She then noticed a tiny tattoo on his wrist, just below the watch but before the hand. It was three initials: B.H.G. For a moment she thought it vaguely familiar. But then Winnie the Mackerel drew her attention back again.

'Ah Agnes, I think you're being a bit hard on him. I think Dermot's just trying to sort himself out and building himself up to it – know what I mean?'

'Not at all! He's a thoughtless, selfish bastard, just like his father was.'

The two women now drew on their cigarettes simultaneously. After exhaling, they both picked up their drinks and took a mouthful. It was like watching people doing synchronised swimming. Arthur, the barman, then arrived at the snug's hatch with a round of drinks.

'Here we are, girls!' he announced as he placed the drinks down on the bar counter.

The two women looked at each other.

'Jesus, Winnie, I didn't see you ordering that!'

'I didn't order it, still I'll pay for it!' and Winnie stood up.

'That's all right, girls, it's already paid for,' Arthur announced, as if he had paid for it himself.

'Paid for by who?' the two women asked in chorus.

'By this man – ah Jaysus, he's gone! The man that was sitting there.'

'Who was he?' Winnie asked.

'I'm not sure. He looked familiar, actually he looked like one of your lads, Agnes. Anyway the drink is paid for.' Arthur was too busy to play detective.

Agnes jumped up and burst through the snug door. All she saw was an empty stool and a half-finished pint of Guinness. Then she remembered the tattoo. It had been applied using the sharp end of a compass and Indian ink. B.H.G. stood for Boot Hill Gang. Suddenly it was clear. Just as suddenly everything went black.

Chapter 25

PROBABLY THE BEST WAY TO EXPLAIN what an aneurysm is, is to imagine the veins as plumber's pipes. Now, try and picture a four-inch pipe coming to a V joint where it divides into two-inch pipes. One can imagine that when the gush of water from the four-inch pipe tries to disperse through the two two-inch pipes the build-up of pressure at the joint can be quite severe. Plumber's pipes are made of copper. Unfortunately veins are not. Aneurysms can occur anywhere in the body, but they are most serious when they are in the brain. When the pressure builds up in an aneurysm it begins to inflate, and this can cause periods of unconsciousness. However, if the joint bursts it causes a cerebral haemorrhage, its most serious consequence. This usually causes brain damage, the symptoms of which are akin to a stroke. Most often indeed an aneurysm *is* followed by a stroke. On some occasions, it can be fatal.

When the ambulance arrived at Madigan's public house the paramedics immediately gave oxygen to Agnes. Then they gently lifted the woman's crumpled body onto a stretcher. The ambulance rushed to the nearest casualty department, which was at the Mater Hospital on the North Circular Road. Winnie the Mackerel telephoned Pierre. Before leaving the house in Wolfe Tone Grove to go to the hospital, a panicking and worried Pierre 'phoned Mark and broke the news to him. Mark immediately dropped everything and prepared to leave for the Mater, instructing his secretary to inform every member of the Browne family of what had happened and where their mother was. Mark then went into the general office of Senga Furnishings where he took Cathy to one side and told her. With Cathy in tears, they left the building and made their way directly to the casualty department of the Mater Hospital. Within forty-five minutes all but two of Agnes Browne's living children were in the waiting room.

In Manchester, Trevor Browne was working on an illustration for his brother Dermot's latest book, *Blue Boy and Mary,* when his studio door opened. He knew immediately he saw Maria's ashen face that something was terribly wrong. Two hours later they were both aboard the *St Finbar,* an Aer Lingus 737, as it took off from Manchester airport. Trevor watched from his window seat as the ground sank away from the aircraft. Maria gently squeezed his hand. He made a great effort to smile, but couldn't.

At half-past eight that same night Buster Brady was sitting in front of the open fire at his home in the gate lodge. Pamela was asleep and Buster was worried. It just wasn't like Cathy not to ring if she was going to be late home. He only barely heard the knock on the door above the racket the rain was making as it lashed against the windows. When he opened the front door Buster was surprised to find young Cormac standing on the doorstep under an umbrella. The boy had no coat on and was shivering.

'Cormac? Come in, son, come in.' Buster took the umbrella from the boy and shook it. He led Cormac into the hallway and closed the door against the rain.

'Dermot said I was to stay here tonight,' Cormac said, his face sad.

'Sure, it will be a pleasure to have you here. Did he say why, Cormac?'

The boy shrugged and shook his head slowly.

Buster squatted down in front of him. 'What's wrong, son?'

'Dermot's up in the house on his own. He's crying ... and he's drunk.' The boy began to sob.

Buster took the boy into a warm embrace and spoke softly into his ear. 'Don't you worry, Cormac. Dermot has a lot on his mind, he probably just needs to be alone tonight. He'll be fine in the morning, you'll see. Come on, let's you and me have a couple of cups of hot chocolate.' He held the boy back at arm's length and beamed a smile at him. 'What do you say?'

Cormac's face brightened a little. 'Okay, Buster, thanks.'

After a cup of hot chocolate, and a long chat which encompassed everything from Cormac's new school to Buster's hopes for his gardening business, Cormac began to feel drowsy. Buster picked up the boy and carried him to his and Cathy's bed where he undressed him and tucked him in. It was an hour later when the phone rang. Buster snatched it up before it had completed its second ring. Slowly Buster sank into the chair beside the hall table as Cathy broke the news, explaining why she was late in coming home.

The rain was now teeming down. Buster ran up the driveway as fast as he could but was still drenched by the time he got to the front door of Dermot's house, which now bore the nameplate 'Dragonfly' in black on brass. Lights were on everywhere in the house. He could hear the strains of Johnny Reggae playing in one of the rooms. It was old 'seventies music and reminded Buster of the days when he and Dermot were skinheads and used to dance to all kinds of reggae. Buster rang on the doorbell. He waited. He rang on the doorbell again, this time four times. Again he waited. Again there was no answer. Getting himself even more wet, and cursing, Buster made his way around to the kitchen door which he found unlocked. When he had closed the door behind him he snatched one of Mrs Dolan's tea-towels and began to dry his hair as he walked through the house.

He found Dermot in the sitting room. The album Dermot had been listening to was finished and the turntable was now making a 'clickety-click' sound, as the needle jumped around the last groove in the album. Dermot was unconscious. He was a mess. The shattered remains of a broken whiskey bottle were strewn around the fireplace. Dermot was lying half-on, half-off the couch, his hand resting on another bottle of whiskey, the contents of which were half-consumed. Buster shook him. Dermot slowly opened his eyes. When he recognised Buster, Dermot's face broke into the lazy, stupid smile of the drunk.

'Ah, Buster ... there you are ... come on and the two of us will rob a bus. Ha, ha, ha!' Dermot's voice was slurred and he broke into a manic laugh as he sat up, or at least tried to sit up.

'Jesus, Dermo, are you all right?' Buster was concerned.

'I'm grand, Buster, fuckin' grand, never felt better in me life. Sure, am I not me father's son and well able for the whiskey?' Dermot held up the half-bottle of whiskey in the air. 'Whiskey is your only man, Buster, will you have some?'

'No thanks, Dermo, I don't want any. Listen, Dermot, I have some bad news –'

'Good man, Buster, just what we need – a little bit o' bad news. Lay it on me – I'm your man for the bad news. Sure, wasn't me father bad news, and amn't I bad news, and no news is good news and ... Oh fuck!' Dermot slumped back down onto the couch.

Buster stretched his arm out and stopped Dermot putting the bottle to his lips. 'Dermo, listen for a second. Your mother's been taken into hospital.'

Dermot had his mouth in an 'O' shape, anticipating it meeting the neck of the bottle. His mouth then changed to a grin. 'Good! I hope it's a fuckin' mental hospital!'

'Dermo, I'm serious.'

'So am I, Buster, dead fuckin' serious. That woman has no time for me – and I have no time for her. And that's the way it is, Buster, no fuckin' time. Do you know what I mean?'

Buster tried again. 'Dermot, I think she might be *really* sick.'

'Buster, I *know* she's really fuckin' sick – sure she's a fuckin' lunatic.'

Dismayed, Buster now tried to lift Dermot to his feet. 'Come on, Dermo, we have to get you to the hospital.'

'I will and me bollox.' Dermot said this with venom, as he pushed Buster back. In his drunken state, Dermot underestimated his own strength. Buster toppled backwards, cracking the side of his head on the corner of the coffee table. Dermot sat back down on the couch. Buster stood up and put his hand to his cheekbone where he had hit his face. When he took his hand away and looked at his fingers there was blood on them.

'I'm cut,' he said simply.

Dermot didn't look over to him, he just took a swig from the whiskey bottle. 'Don't worry, you'll fuckin' heal.' Dermot lay back and closed his eyes.

Buster had had enough. He turned and walked out of the room. As he opened the front door to leave, the telephone began to ring. He heard Dermot answer it.

'What d'you want?' Dermot roared into the mouthpiece. It was Mark calling from the hospital. He was calling to tell Dermot where Agnes was and what was happening. Buster had closed the door and was taking his first steps back into the rain when he heard Dermot's roar.

'Fuck off!' The telephone came crashing through the window. Buster pulled up his collar and headed back to the gate lodge.

Mark had insisted that Agnes be taken from casualty to a private room. The doctor treating Agnes had asked the nurse to gather all of her family into one of the small waiting rooms where he would then be able to speak to them in private. This was where they now all sat in silence, awaiting the doctor's arrival. A nurse sat on a chair just inside the door and when the door opened she was expecting it to be the doctor. It wasn't. It was another man. One she did not recognise. She stood up, blocking his entry.

'I'm sorry, this room is for family only,' she said in a friendly but firm tone as she pushed her hand against the man's chest.

From behind the nurse it was Mark that spoke. 'Excuse me, nurse! He *is* family.'

The nurse apologised and held the door open. Dino Doyle smiled a 'thanks' to Mark and made his way to Rory's side. The two men looked at each other for a moment without speaking, then Rory began to cry. Dino gently laid Rory's head on his shoulder and started to stroke his head to comfort him.

When the doctor walked in the door Pierre stood up. The doctor extended his hand. 'Mr Browne?' the doctor asked.

'No, Mr Du Gloss. I am Mrs Browne's partner.'

'Oh I see, please do sit down.' The doctor sat at the only table in the waiting room. The gathering waited expectantly.

'I wish I was the bearer of better news,' the doctor began. 'Our scan shows a cerebral haemorrhage, caused by an aneurysm. Now, before you ask me all the obvious questions, let me explain that there is no particular reason for this. People are born with aneurysms. Some people born with aneurysms go through their whole lives never being affected by them, or even knowing that they have one. In other cases people *are* affected by them and recover. But I must be honest here, in a lot of cases they can cause a stroke – and even be fatal.'

The doctor waited, nobody asked a question, so he went on. 'The first thing we are doing now is trying to relieve the swelling on the brain. It worries me a little that your mother hasn't regained consciousness yet. However, even if she does I must warn you that we will be keeping her sedated for some time yet. The next twenty-four hours will be crucial, we will just all have to wait and see what happens.'

With the exception of sniffles from Rory, Fiona and Betty, everyone was silent. Cathy slowly put her hand up as if in class.

'Yes?' the doctor asked.

'Is it all right if we sit with her?'

'Of course it is, in fact it's good for you all to be here. If she does come out it will help her to see her family's faces. And if she doesn't, well ...' the doctor left his sentence unfinished. Then he stood up and went to leave, but he stopped in front of Pierre. 'Mr du Gloss, I'm available if you have any questions at any time,' and he extended his hand again.

Pierre again stood up and shook the man's hand. 'Thank you, doctor, thank you very much.' Pierre spoke warmly but weakly.

*   *   *

When Dermot awoke the next morning he was freezing cold. He had been lying beneath the broken window. Although it had stopped raining outside, it had rained long enough during the night for the carpet, the couch – and indeed Dermot – to be drenched from the rain that had been blowing through the broken window. He got up gingerly. His head was pounding and he felt nauseous. Tottering like a crotchety old man he made his way to the kitchen and delved into the fridge for a carton of orange juice. He gulped it down quickly in an effort to quell his thirst and remove the filthy taste from his mouth. He put the kettle on, then went to the medicine chest and got himself two Solpadeine tablets. He gagged as he tried to down the half-glass of water containing the soluble tablets. When the kettle was boiled he made himself a cup of instant coffee. Carrying the cup, he made his way back into the sitting room. The place was a mess. He saw some blood on the edge of the coffee table and spots of it on the carpet. He examined himself thoroughly and could find no cuts. There was broken glass everywhere – around the fireplace from the broken bottle, and all over the room where the rain and wind had blown pieces in from the broken window. He looked out through the shattered window frame. The telephone was sitting on the bonnet of his car.

'What the fuck?' He massaged his eyes and made his way back into the kitchen where he sat and held his head in his hands. After a while, he didn't know how long, he heard the front door open and close and the sound of Mrs Dolan shaking off her coat.

'Sweet loving Jesus!' she screamed.

She arrived at the kitchen door holding Cormac by the hand. The boy looked terrified.

'Oh Christ!' Dermot exclaimed, as he tried to hide his face.

'Well now ... you must be very proud of yourself this morning, Mr Browne!' Mrs Dolan chastised him, and she looked furious.

'What's the boy doing here?' Dermot said from under his arm.

'He lives here, or did you forget that, along with the fact that you are supposed to be a gentleman?'

'I mean, how did you get him?'

'Mr Brady dropped him into my house this morning on his way in to the hospital. He's gone to see *your* mother apparently. Did you know your mother was in hospital?' Mrs Dolan now sounded more like a schoolteacher than a housekeeper.

Dermot spoke again without lifting his head. 'Yes.'

'Then one would wonder why you aren't visiting your mother?'

Dermot now lifted his head and rose from the chair, squaring up to Mrs Dolan. '*One* might be better off ... minding one's own fuckin' business, Mrs Dolan!' Dermot had had enough.

'Well, my God!' the woman exclaimed as she stomped out of the kitchen. Soon, Dermot could hear her noisily rooting in the cupboards of the utility room to get out her cleaning materials. She began to clear up the mess. Dermot had sat back down again at the kitchen table. Without speaking, Cormac put on the kettle and took his father's mug from his hand. He rinsed the mug under the tap and made his father another cup of coffee. Carrying it carefully across the floor, the boy gently placed it in front of his father. Then he too sat at the kitchen table. During all of this Cormac didn't speak once. Dermot took a sip of the coffee.

'I'm sorry about last night, Cormac.' Dermot was embarrassed.

'It's okay.'

'No, it's not okay. I shouldn't have behaved like that. I won't do it again.'

'No, really, it is okay. Buster explained everything.' The boy seemed confident that he knew exactly what was going on.

Dermot stared at the boy. 'Did he now? And what exactly did Buster explain?'

'That you have a lot of pain inside you. Old memories that aren't nice. And that some people try to kill the pain with drink. And that even though you knew that didn't work, you had to try it anyway, you had to find out for yourself. That's what Buster said.'

Dermot dropped his head onto his arm again. 'Jesus Christ, maybe it's Buster that should be writing the fuckin' books,' Dermot mumbled. Slowly he rose from the table and began to make his way to the stairs. On the way he went into the sitting room and tried to apologise to Mrs Dolan.

'Er ... Mrs Dolan, I'm sorry ... I, er ... well, I'm sorry.'

'And so you *should be*, young man,' Mrs Dolan replied as she turned her back and carried on with her cleaning. She wasn't giving in yet.

Dermot felt better after a shower and a shave. He put on some fresh clothes and when he came downstairs Mrs Dolan was busy with the hoover. Cormac was still sitting at the kitchen table.

'Do you want to go down and play with Pamela?' Dermot asked Cormac.

'Pamela's not there. She's gone in with Buster, to the hospital.'

'Oh right. I'll tell you what, why don't you and me go out and get something to eat somewhere and leave Mrs Dolan alone. We only seem to be in the way, and I seem to be really annoying her.' Without trying to court any more favour from Mrs Dolan, Dermot quietly left with the boy.

*   *   *

180

It had been Betty's idea to bring the children. At first Mark was against it.

'No, no – a hospital is not the place for children, not when their granny is like this,' he argued.

'Well, I'd feel better if Aaron was here, and I've spoken to Fiona and Cathy and they agree.'

'I know it sounds like a good idea, darling, but –'

Before Mark could finish Pierre interrupted. 'It is not my place to say it, they are your children, but Agnes has always loved the sound of children's voices and their laughter. Perhaps it would be good to have them here?'

Mark thought for a moment. 'Yes ... you two are right, go on, Betty, get the kids – and, Pierre, it *is* your place to say it. Our children look on you as their grandfather, you know, just as much as we look on you as a father.'

Pierre smiled. 'Thank you, Mark.'

Betty and Fiona went home for their children. Cathy called Buster and asked him to come in along with Pamela. Within an hour the room was alive with chattering children. There is no doubt that the presence of the children brightened everyone a little and the tone of everybody's voice changed to normal conversation from what had previously been just whispers.

*　　*　　*

Agnes Browne wasn't sure what was happening. Everything was dark at first. Then she could see a tiny light just like a pinprick. Gradually the light got bigger and bigger and bigger. For some time she stared at the light. It was nice, warm and friendly. Then she heard a voice she recognised. It was singing.

'When no-one else can understand, ooh, wooh wooh,
When everything I do is wrong ...'

'Marion? Is that you, Marion?'

'Ah, Agnes, how are you, love?'

It was indeed the voice of Marion Monks, Agnes's best
friend and companion for many, many years. From her
childhood up till Marion's untimely death in 1967, Agnes
could not remember a time when Marion Monks was not
by her side.

'What's happening, Marion, what's happening to me?'

'I've come to show you the way, Agnes. Just put your
hand out into the darkness and I'll take it.'

'Show me the way to where, Marion?'

'To where you're goin', Agnes. To here.'

Agnes thought for a moment and then it dawned on
her.

'Oh – THERE.'

'Now you have it, Agnes, are yeh right? Come on.'

'What's it like? Marion, what's it like ... there?'

'It's only brilliant, Agnes, you're goin' to love it. Bingo
every night. As much cider as you want. And real inter-
esting people too. I had dinner with Elvis last week.'

'Would you fuck off, Marion Monks. What would Elvis
be doing with you?'

Marion's laughter was sweet and musical. 'Ah janey,
Agnes, you haven't changed a bit. God, I've missed you.'

'Not as much as I've missed you, Marion.'

'Then come on, will yeh? Don't be keepin' me waitin'.'

'Marion?'

'Yeh, Agnes?'

'Marion ... is Francis there?'

182

'Frankie? Yeh, 'course he is, Agnes. Now, come on, will yeh?'

'I can't Marion, I can't go yet.'

'Why not?'

'It's not finished – not yet.'

'What's not finished, Agnes, for God's sake?'

'I don't know ... something's not finished ... I've somethin' to do, I don't know what it is ... but I've somethin' to do, Marion. Jesus, Marion, I want to go but I can't, not yet!'

'It's up to you, Agnes. I think you're mad. Ah janey, I wouldn't be able for all that shite again, but it's up to you.' Marion was very matter-of-fact.

'Can I think about it, Marion?'

'Of course you can, Agnes, take as long as you like. Listen, I have to go. I'm doin' a bit of cleanin' for John F Kennedy.'

'Are you, Marion?' Agnes was impressed.

'No, I'm only jokin',' and Marion burst into laughter which faded as the light went out.

Although Agnes was back in the darkness again she was sure she could hear children's voices in the distance.

Chapter 26

'GOD, IT MUST HAVE BEEN A VERY STORMY NIGHT!' Dermot exclaimed as he manoeuvred the car around the pools of water on the road that were caused by overflowing ditches. There were broken branches and pieces of debris all over the road too.

'It was. I couldn't sleep with the thunder and lightning,' Cormac answered.

They were heading down the Dublin road from Kilbride, but when they got to the junction at Mulhuddart, there were bollards blocking their way and an orange sign with the word 'Diversion' on it. Alongside it was a piece of wood which looked like a bread-board. Painted on it by hand were the words: 'Road flooded'.

'Shite!' Dermot exclaimed as he swung the car to the left and down a by-road. Two miles of twisting country road brought them to another main road. There was a lot of traffic on this road and it took Dermot a good two minutes before he was able to swing out into the line of cars. They were now on the Derry to Dublin road, heading for Dublin. This road would bring them straight past Finglas, Dermot's old home. As they approached Finglas, the road became a modern highway which hadn't been there when Dermot had left Ireland. Looking out to each side of the motorway he recognised streets and factories from his childhood years. He suddenly brought the car to a stop.

'What's wrong?' Cormac asked.

Dermot was staring out the driver's window.

'Nothing's wrong.' Dermot continued to stare. For a few moments Cormac sat twiddling his thumbs. Then he knelt up on the passenger's seat and, looking over his father's shoulder, asked, 'Why are we stopped?'

Dermot pointed, his finger up against the window. 'Can you see that big chestnut tree over there?' he asked Cormac.

The boy followed the line of Dermot's finger and eventually his eyes fell upon what was, right enough, a huge chestnut tree.

'Yes, what about it?' he asked.

'*That*, my son, is Chestnut Hole!'

'Chestnut Hole? Like from the book?' Cormac was getting excited.

'I'm nearly sure it is – I think so anyway.' Dermot too was a little excited.

'Can we go over, can we go over and look, see if we can find Chestnut Hole?' Cormac was tugging at the door handle on the passenger side of the car.

Dermot smiled. 'Yeh, come on. Why not!'

Dermot took the boy by the hand and they carefully crossed the dual carriageway. On the far side of the road Dermot lifted the child over a small fence, climbed over it himself, and the two began to trudge across the field.

'This is exciting, isn't it, Dermot?'

'Yes, it is,' Dermot replied, although he sounded more scared than excited now. As they moved farther into the field the ground became wetter and swampy. Dermot stopped.

'Christ, we're going to get ourselves destroyed! Come on, let's go back.'

'Oh no, Dermot, don't go back now, I want to see Chestnut Hole, please!'

Dermot looked at the boy. Then he looked up at the chestnut tree. They were no more than a hundred yards from it. Maybe it was the drink from the night before, but his stomach felt sick, and his hands began to shake. When he answered the boy there was a tremor in his voice.

'Okay, then, let's go.' They went on. They reached the tree in a few seconds, both now up to their knees in mud. It was a good ten minutes more before they found the entrance to Chestnut Hole. It was Dermot who found it.

'Cormac! Over here, son, I think I've found it!'

He waited for Cormac to join him. Then together they scurried through the entrance into the ancient hut. Dermot took out his lighter and flicked it. The hut lit up. In the centre of the floor were the remains of a small fire, and neatly piled in one corner were four candles. It was obvious that Chestnut Hole had now acquired new residents and had become the headquarters of some new Boot Hill Gang of the nineties. Dermot was glad. He picked up two candles and handed one to Cormac. He lit them and they looked around. Memories came flooding back to Dermot and he began to give the boy a guided tour.

'Just over there,' he pointed to one corner, 'is where I had my seat. We had two seats. We got them out of an old Austin Cambridge; one was Buster's, one was mine. I had mine over there.' Dermot turned. 'Buster had his over here. And see where that fire is now? That's where we used to lay out our mattress on nights when we slept here.'

'It looks like somebody else has moved in,' Cormac commented.

'Yes, it does,' Dermot answered. They moved the candles around to try and see every inch of the place, and there was no talking for a while.

Then young Cormac, standing in the middle of the hut, took a deep breath and exclaimed, 'This place is really great, Daddy.'

Not since the day Dermot had taken Cormac from Margaret O'Brien's house had the child ever, not even by accident, called Dermot 'Daddy'. The boy hadn't even noticed it now, but Dermot was nearly floored.

'Yes, son, there's a kind of magic here all right!' Dermot answered, slowly looking around, and the words seemed vaguely familiar to him. Suddenly a thought struck him and he clicked his fingers. 'I bet the new tenants haven't found my hidey hole.' Dermot began to move the candle along the wall looking for the loose brick. He tried one or two; when a brick didn't budge immediately he knew it wasn't his hidey hole. When eventually he found it, he started to wriggle the brick out of place. It was heavier than he remembered and it slipped from his fingers and fell to the ground with a thud. Dermot jumped back. Cormac stood on the brick and looked into the hidey hole.

'Hey! There's something in here,' Cormac announced as he delved his hand into the hole. When his hand reappeared, there was an envelope in it. Cormac examined it with wide, excited eyes. Written on the envelope was the name *Dermot Browne.*

'It's a letter! And it's for you, Daddy.' He handed it to Dermot.

'What?' Dermot was dumbfounded. He squatted, stuck the candle into the soft clay floor and began to open the letter. The envelope was wet and very old and as he tried to pull it open, it came apart in his hands. There was what looked like a note inside. It had been folded in three and Dermot tried to peel it apart gently. By the time he had it fully open it was torn, and between dampness and age most of the words were illegible. But Dermot could make out the beginning and the end of the note. The opening words were:

'My dearest Dermot, I am so sorry ...'

and the closing words were:

'... that wherever you go I will always be proud of you. You are in my prayers and in my thoughts always. Love, Mammy.'

Dermot sank slowly into a sitting position. As he did, his hands came apart and the damp piece of paper broke apart. Between the thumb and forefinger of his left hand he held a piece of paper that read, *'Dear Dermot,'* and between the forefinger and thumb of his right hand a piece of paper that read, *'Love, Mammy.'* He didn't cry.

'Are you okay, Daddy?' Cormac asked, concerned.

'I'm fine, son,' Dermot answered, and he stood up. He placed the two small pieces of damp paper one into each of his jacket pockets. Then he took the boy's hand and said, 'Come on, Cormac, we have to get to the hospital.'

An hour later the new tenants of Chestnut Hole arrived to find two candles burning in the middle of their hut. They were sure the place had been visited by a ghost. They weren't far off.

*   *   *

Dermot and Cormac, hand-in-hand, walked along the corridor toward Agnes Browne's room, leaving muddy footprints on the shiny marble floor behind them. As they approached the private room in which Dermot's mother lay, the door opened and Mark stepped out into the corridor. Dermot stopped. Mark walked towards him. Dermot didn't know what kind of reaction to expect from Mark, so he was ready for anything. When the estranged brothers were standing face-to-face Dermot searched for a clue in Mark's eyes.

'Welcome home, brother,' Mark said with a smile, and opened his arms for a hug. Dermot fell into his arms. It was a long hug. Both men kept their eyes closed. When they separated, Dermot began to speak.

'How is me Mammy?'

'Still in a coma,' Mark answered evenly.

Dermot looked at the floor. 'Look, Mark, I've been a bit of an asshole –'

Mark interrupted with a wave of his hand. He put his arm around his brother's shoulder. 'Look, Dermot, what's gone is gone, let's not look back. It's just good to have you here, it will mean so much to Mammy – it means so much to all of us.'

'Thanks,' was all Dermot could say for fear that if he went any further he would surely cry.

'So, *you're* Cormac?' Mark crouched beside the boy. 'Well, Cormac, I'm your Uncle Mark, son, and behind that door you're about to meet more uncles and aunties than you can shake a stick at!' Mark smiled at the boy and the boy smiled back.

Dermot was overwhelmed at the welcome he received when he stepped into his mother's room. The gap in his life had been bridged with the solid steel of love. When the welcomes died down, Dermot moved to his mother's bedside. Agnes's dark skin looked sallow rather than pale and she looked like she was just in a deep sleep. Dermot took her hand and held it between both of his. Unabashed, he began to speak to his mother, and as he did the family gathered round the bed.

'Mammy ... it's me, Dermot. I just want you to know that I'm home safe and sound ... and that I love you.'

It was short and sweet, but the relief that overcame Dermot was incredible. He felt as if a truck had been parked on his chest for ten years and now suddenly somebody had moved it – it was gone! He smiled. All of the Brownes smiled.

*   *   *

Agnes saw the light begin to appear again. Its increase in size was rapid this time. As she expected, along with the light came Marion's voice.

　'Yoo hoo! Agnes – I'm back!'
　'Howyeh, Marion? I missed you, where were you?'
　'I was out for me jog.'

'Jog, me arse! Sure, you'd run out of breath jogging your feckin' memory!'

The two women laughed.

'Ah, you wouldn't know me now, Agnes – a body like Brigitte Bardot.'

'Bridget the Midget you mean?' And again the two women laughed.

'God, Marion ... I really have missed you.'

'And I've missed you too, Agnes.'

'Marion, why can't I see you?'

"'Cause you haven't crossed over. It's a rule they have here, you have to cross over. It's a load of shite if you ask me, but there you are, rules is rules! Agnes, if you just put your hand out into the dark I'll take it and I'll bring you over.'

'I can't, Marion, not yet ... Marion, can you hear children's voices?'

There was quiet for a moment.

'No. They must be on your side, I can't hear them. Now look, Agnes, are you coming or what?' Marion was getting impatient.

'Marion, just give me a few more minutes, will you? Just a few more minutes to make up me mind, please, will you?'

'All right then. See you later, alligator.' Marion began to sing and her voice faded away.

*   *   *

Once again Agnes was alone in the darkness. Again she heard the children's voices, but this time louder. Also she thought she could feel something in her hand. It felt like ... another hand, a child's hand. She tried desperately to open her eyes. Slowly there came a light – not like Marion's light, this time it was a dim light. The light became a haze and in the haze she could make out shapes. People. As the haze began to clear a little she could clearly make out faces. She looked at the faces. They were all standing around her bed. Mark and Betty with Aaron. Simon and Fiona with Thomas. Trevor and Maria, Cathy and Buster with Pamela. Rory – and Dino! She was glad. Pierre, oh Pierre. This man she loved more than any man she had ever held in her arms. Little Cormac? She could feel her heart begin to shudder, and standing beside Cormac was the owner of the hand that was holding hers. It was another little boy almost identical to Cormac. It was Dermot. But Dermot is a man, she thought. She looked harder, she could see the shape of the man but much more clearly from out of that shape was a little boy holding her hand. Her heart began to sing. The effort of trying to see was tiring her so she sank back into the darkness again, except this time she felt complete. Whole!

'Her eyes moved.' It was Cormac who spoke.

'What, son?' Dermot asked.

'I said her eyes moved, Daddy. Granny – her eyes moved. It was just a flicker, but they moved.'

Dermot gently placed his mother's hand back on the bed, he sat down on a chair and lifted his son onto his lap.

'Of course they did, son, of course they did.' He hugged the boy.

'What do we do now, Daddy?' Cormac asked.

'We wait, son. We pray – and we wait.'

It was at three o'clock on the afternoon of 6 December 1992, with, for the first time in fifteen years, every single living member of her family gathered around her, united, that Agnes Browne smiled and became a dragonfly.